The
Scariest
Night

ALSO BY BETTY REN WRIGHT

Christina's Ghost

The Dollhouse Murders

A Ghost in the Window

The Ghost of Ernie P.

Ghosts Beneath Our Feet

The Midnight Mystery
(original title: *Rosie and the Dance of the Dinosaurs*)

The Pike River Phantom

The Secret Window

The Summer of Mrs. MacGregor

The Scariest Night

Betty Ren Wright

AN
APPLE
PAPERBACK

SCHOLASTIC INC.
New York Toronto London Auckland Sydney

ISBN 0-590-45918-X

12 11 10 9 8 7 6 5 4 3 2   3 4 5 6 7 8/9

Printed in the U.S.A.   28

First Scholastic printing, August 1993

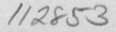

For
ROBERT W. SWAIN,
Uncle Bob

The
Scariest
Night

Chapter One

"He's not here!" Erin Lindsay's voice spiraled upward. She was on her knees, hunched next to an overflowing shopping bag and searching under the driver's seat in front of her. She felt a pink plastic lipstick. A map of Wisconsin. An empty soda can. No cat.

"Of course he's here," her mother said. "He has to be. Keep looking."

"He's not!" Erin shoved her foster brother's feet out of the way and reached under the seat on the passenger's side. A book of ghost stories. A Styrofoam cup. A music magazine. No cat.

She straightened up. "He's really not here," she repeated, too frightened to cry. "You opened the window back there at the gas station, Cowbird. I told you not to, but you did. And Rufus got out!".

"I didn't," Cowper said uneasily. But from the way he answered, Erin knew she was right. When he didn't complain about her calling him Cowbird instead of Cowper, he had to be guilty.

"It's your own fault for letting him out of his travel case," he protested. "We might have died sitting in the car with all the windows closed and no air conditioning."

"It's not my fault we're traveling a million miles on the hottest day of the year," Erin retorted. "Poor Rufus was *dying* in his case."

"Now stop that," Mrs. Lindsay said sharply. "Rufus was perfectly all right where he was, Erin. If he's lost, you'll have to take part of the blame."

"Daddy—" Erin leaned forward.

"I'm already looking for a place to turn around," her father said. He sounded tired. "I've been looking for the last five miles. I just wish you'd noticed before that he was missing. It's been twenty minutes since we left that gas station. By this time . . ."

He didn't finish the sentence, but Erin knew what could have happened by this time. Rufus seldom went outside their yard at home in Clinton. He didn't know what could happen to a cat on the highway. He didn't know about cat-nappers. He didn't know about mean dogs. By this time he could be lying somewhere in a ditch. She might never hold him again and pet him and listen to the Rufus-purr that was almost a growl.

Erin threw herself back in the seat, aware that Cowper was watching her uneasily. "If Rufus is gone," she mouthed the words so that her parents wouldn't hear, "I'll never forgive you. Not ever."

Cowper looked out the window, his round face set in tight lines. *As if he cares!* Erin thought.

They rode in silence for a few minutes, and then Erin's father said something else that made her stomach turn over. "The filling station's just around the next curve. Keep your eyes open. Erin, you watch one side of the road, and Cowper, you watch the other. Rufus may have started out on his own."

And been hit by a car! Erin pressed her forehead against the glass. *Don't let him be lying there,* she prayed. *Let him be walking along, looking for us.*

The gas station was on a slope, set back from the highway. Two huge semitrailer trucks filled the entrance, blocking their way.

"Blow the horn, Daddy," Erin said. "Make them move."

Her mother shook her head. "Honestly, Erin, you're going to be a terrible driver someday. You can't just go around blasting people out of your way. There must be some good reason why those trucks have stopped. Be patient."

Erin couldn't bear it. She threw open the door and slid out before her parents could stop her.

"I'll go with her," Cowper said, scrambling after

her. *Trying to make up,* she thought, and hurried up the blacktop past the trucks.

The driver of the first truck was out of his cab and looking down at something on the road. Two other men were standing with him. Erin caught a glimpse of orange-red fur at their feet.

"No!" she wailed. "Oh no!"

The truck driver turned around, and then Erin saw Rufus, his back arched, his tail three times its normal size. His lips were pulled back and he was hissing like a snake.

"Rufus!" Erin smiled and ran to him. "Oh, baby! I'm so glad you're safe."

The driver stepped back. "He yours, kid? Good thing you got here when you did. One more minute with this four-legged roadblock and I was going to flatten him with my rig. This here's the stubbornnest beast I ever met."

"He's not stubborn!" Erin said. She gathered Rufus into her arms and cradled him. "He's just frightened half to death. What would *you* do if a great big truck was coming at you?"

"I'd move," the driver said, and the other men laughed. Behind her, Erin heard Cowper snicker.

"He was too scared to move!" Erin exclaimed. Rufus peered over her arm and began his purr-growl. "You should have just picked him up like this and—"

"Picked him up!" the driver exclaimed. "I'd rather pick up a rattlesnake. Now if you'll clear the road . . ."

Erin darted back to the car, with Cowper right behind her. They climbed in, and Mr. Lindsay backed up and turned the car around.

"Well, thank goodness, that's over," Mrs. Lindsay said. "Put the cat in his case, Erin. It's safer."

"You should have seen him." Cowper chuckled. "He wasn't going to get out of the way for anybody. If we hadn't come back, they'd probably have had to close up the gas station for the day."

"That's silly," Erin said. She dropped Rufus into his case on the seat between them and closed the door. "Don't you mind, baby," she crooned. "Pretty soon we'll be in Milwaukee, and then you can run and play."

"And that's another thing," Mrs. Lindsay said, as if she'd just been reviewing a whole string of problems. "We don't know how that cat is going to take to apartment living."

"We don't know how any of us will take to apartment living," Mr. Lindsay commented. "I've only been inside an apartment building a few times in my life. But we'll get used to it, I guess. We'll manage. It's just for the summer, after all, and it's for a great cause." He winked at Cowper in the rearview mirror.

"I'd rather be home in Clinton," Erin said. "A billion times rather!"

She laid a hand on the case so that Rufus could sniff her fingers through the wires. Then she looked at Cowper—his short, round body, his shining glasses, the blank look he'd put on like a mask now that they were on their way again.

It's his summer, Erin thought crossly. He was the one who mattered. She'd suspected it for a long time, but she hadn't been sure until her parents announced that they were going to move to the city for the summer so Cowper could take a master class in piano. Cowbird the wonderboy!

She sighed. This was supposed to have been the Great Shake-and-Shiver Summer of Horrors. She and Heather and Emily and Meg had been planning it for months. First they were going to explore the old haunted schoolhouse south of Clinton. Then they were going to rent the best ghost-and-horror videos they could find. They were going to spend whole nights in Heather's tent in Heather's backyard telling stories about witches and werewolves.

The Great Shake-and-Shiver Summer of Horrors. Erin had named it and planned it. And now it was all going to happen without her.

Chapter Two

Erin had been trying to be a good person for as long as she could remember. Three years ago she'd put aside her favorite mysteries and ghost stories to read a book called *A Little Princess*. Then and there, the heroine, Sara Crewe, had become her ideal. Sara was very rich, but she didn't act as if she thought she was better than anyone else. She shared her riches with her friends at boarding school, and she tried to make everyone as happy as she was.

Then Sara's father died, and she discovered that all his money had been invested in a diamond mine that hadn't produced any diamonds. Overnight, Sara became the poorest girl in the school. The headmistress let her stay on, since she had nowhere else to go, but now she was the servant girl who had to scrub floors and make beds and wash dishes all day. Some of the students, the ones who had been secretly jealous, were cruel to her, but Sara stayed as sweet and good as ever. She was perfect.

Erin read *A Little Princess* four times. In some mysterious way, Sara Crewe became a part of her. Not that she wanted to *be* Sara, a lonely orphan in turn-of-the-century England. She had enjoyed being Erin Lindsay, the much-loved only child of schoolteacher parents. But to be good and sweet and kind like Sara, no matter what happened—that would be wonderful. It hadn't seemed so hard until Cowper became part of the family.

Now, as the car rolled through the outskirts of Milwaukee, past endless acres of one-story factories and motels and parking lots, Erin tried to think Sara Crewe thoughts. After all, Rufus was safe in his carrying case once more, none the worse for his adventure. And Cowper hadn't let him out of the car on purpose.

Cowper's just a little kid, Erin's Sara Crewe self said firmly. *Nine is a baby compared to twelve. So forget it!* But forgetting wasn't that easy. Cowper might be just a little kid, but he was running their lives.

Without wanting to, Erin recalled the day, two years ago, when Cowper moved into the Lindsays' spare bedroom. His mother and father had been killed in a car crash the night before, and the Lindsays, his parents' best friends, had tried in every way to comfort him. Erin remembered those first few days vividly. Cowper had clung to her mother but had hardly answered when they tried to talk to him. When Erin offered to play a board game or take him up to her treehouse, he had shaken his head and turned away. Most of the time he sat at the Lindsays' seldom-used piano, just staring at the music as if he could hear it by looking at it.

"He's a spooky little kid," Erin said one day when she and her mother were frosting sugar cookies. Her mother's reply had changed her whole life.

"Cowper is a genius, dear. That makes him different from the rest of us, not spooky. Raising a child like Cowper will be a big responsibility. His parents devoted their lives to him. I hope we're up to it."

Erin froze. "You mean he's going to stay?" She'd been making a face on a cookie, using M&M candies, and one brown eye stared up at her as she tried to take in what her mother had just said.

"He needs us." Mrs. Lindsay spoke slowly, carefully. "Think how you'd feel if you lost Dad and me. Put yourself in Cowper's shoes. He'll keep his own name— Cowper Williams—that's only fair to his parents. He can go on calling us Aunt Grace and Uncle Jack, the way he always has. But from now on he'll be our little boy and your brother."

Erin stared down at the table. She knew what Sara Crewe would do. She'd say, "How wonderful to have a little brother!" Then she'd find Cowper and give him a big hug and welcome him to the family. But Erin Lindsay didn't want to do any of those things. She wanted to run to her bedroom and slam the door and cry for hours.

She hadn't done any of those things either. In the end, she'd just stood there saying nothing. After a while she found another chocolate M&M and gave the cookie a second eye.

"I've always wished you had a brother or sister," her mother went on. "An only child can have a lonely time of it."

"I'm not lonely," Erin protested, but something— maybe it was Sara Crewe—had stopped her from saying more. It wouldn't have made a difference anyway. She knew Cowper was there to stay, and nothing would ever be the same again.

"Here's our exit ramp." Mr. Lindsay swung the car expertly into a steeply sloping turnoff. The freeway was left behind, and they plunged into a bustling city street. Mrs. Lindsay wrinkled her nose.

"It takes a little getting used to," Mr. Lindsay said apologetically. "After a while you won't notice the exhaust fumes."

Erin thought her father sounded like a tour guide. Well, he'd never convince *her* that Milwaukee was a better place to live in than Clinton. Clinton had Market Park, with a swimming pool and a skateboard ramp. The Mississippi River was just a few miles away.

From the Lindsays' house on Robertson Street you could walk to the Dairy Queen and the library and the movie theater. Friends were close by.

What are Heather and Emily and Meg doing right this minute? With a pang, Erin realized she knew exactly what they were doing. Today was the day they'd planned to bike out to the haunted schoolhouse on the edge of town. In the evening they were going to a double-feature horror show at the Capitol, then to Heather's house for the first tent sleepover.

It was going to be the scariest night of my life, Erin thought mournfully. She wondered if her friends were missing her as much as she missed them. Probably not. They had each other.

"Where's the conservatory?" It was the first time Cowper had spoken since they left the gas station. His eyes were anxious behind his glasses.

"It's east of here," Mr. Lindsay said. "A beautiful old building right on the Lake Michigan shore. We'll search it out during the next few days, after we're settled. You don't have to worry about getting there, buddy," he added. "I'll take you until we find out about bus connections."

"I don't think the bus is a good idea at all," Mrs. Lindsay said. She was looking at the traffic with a frightened expression. "We can take you over there on the mornings you have your class."

"I'll have to go every day," Cowper said in his funny,

flat way. "I'll have to practice at the school because there's no piano in the apartment."

"Then we'll take you every day."

Erin bit her lip. Somewhere in this huge, noisy city there was a beautiful old building with a practice room and a piano waiting for her foster brother. There were teachers eager to tell him how special he was. The Lindsays had been in Milwaukee for barely five minutes, but Cowbird already belonged there.

"Watch for Kirby Avenue, folks." Erin's father squinted into the late-afternoon sun. "It has to be pretty close now."

"That was it," Cowper announced a moment later. "We just passed it. I didn't see the street sign, but there was a Kirby Market on the corner."

"Are you sure?" Mrs. Lindsay sounded uneasy. "That didn't look like a street where people *live*."

She was right, Erin decided, when they had circled the block. Shabby little stores, bars, and, most of all, empty lots—that was Kirby Avenue. Here and there a tired-looking office building towered over its neighbors and peered down at them through dusty windows.

"It'll get better," Mr. Lindsay promised. "Nineteen twenty is still a few blocks north."

They rode in silence. Fourteen hundred, fifteen hundred—it didn't get any better.

"Oh, there's the YWCA," Mrs. Lindsay said

brightly. "Erin, they'll probably have some summer activities you'll enjoy while we're at the university." Both Mr. and Mrs. Lindsay planned to take summer school courses during their stay in the city.

Erin glanced at the big gray building without interest. She couldn't imagine herself going through those huge doors and signing up for a class with a lot of strangers. At home she knew people wherever she went.

"Hey, look at this!" Cowper exclaimed as Kirby Avenue angled left around a warehouse and presented them with a new view. "It's like a scene in a war movie."

"Good heavens!" Mrs. Lindsay stopped trying to sound cheerful. "Jack, are you sure you have the right address?"

For at least six blocks ahead and two blocks on either side, every building but one had been torn down. The remaining structure stood like a lighthouse in a sea of vacant lots and crumbling foundations.

"That *can't* be our building," Mrs. Lindsay said. "It isn't, is it, Jack?"

"That's the nineteen hundred block," Cowper reported. "I've been counting."

Mr. Lindsay cleared his throat. "Ken Krueger did say something about a new expressway coming through his neighborhood," he said uneasily. "He mentioned there were going to be a lot of changes, and he'd be making a move before long. But I had no idea . . ."

"A lot of changes," Mrs. Lindsay repeated. "I'd call that the understatement of the year. Cowper is right— it looks as if someone has tried to bomb the whole street off the face of the earth."

The car slid to a stop across from the remaining building. Rufus mewed unhappily from inside his travel case as if he shared the Lindsays' shock.

"It's like an old castle," Erin blurted. "All that carving and the fancy doorway. But nobody lives there, do they? They couldn't!" The battered-looking old building made her shiver. Nothing good could happen there.

Cowper pointed. "Curtains on the windows."

"Well, *we* can't live in a place like that," Mrs. Lindsay said. "I wouldn't feel safe for a minute."

Erin took a deep breath. Maybe they'd be back in Clinton much sooner than she'd thought.

An old man came out of the apartment building and started down the street, pulling a flimsy grocery cart behind him. The Lindsays watched him, not speaking. At last Mr. Lindsay turned around, his expression a mixture of disappointment and determination.

"Before we give up, we'd better keep one thing in mind," he said solemnly. "Ken Krueger's charging us very little—I can see why now—and if we go looking for another apartment we'll have to pay three or four times as much. That's out of the question. We can go in and look around, or we can start for home right now and forget the master class and summer school. It's as simple as that." He paused. "Ken is a cautious soul. I know he wouldn't stay here if he thought the building or the neighborhood was dangerous."

No one said anything for a minute. Then Mrs. Lindsay opened her door. "We might as well look, I guess," she said. "We can't just drive away."

Erin heard Cowper let out his breath. He wanted to go in as much as she didn't want to. She was the only one who believed—and she was absolutely sure of it now—something unpleasant waited for the Lindsays in that building.

They got out of the car and trailed across the street, Erin clutching Rufus's travel case. A half-dozen concrete steps led to a door framed by concrete pillars. Stone lions with chipped faces crouched on either side of the top steps.

Inside, the "castle" was much less grand. A small, dim foyer had a row of mailboxes and call-buttons on one side and a scarred wooden bench on the other. The air was musty.

Mr. Lindsay examined the call-buttons. Only about half of the buttons had tenants' names lettered next to them.

"Grady," he read aloud. "Superintendent." He lifted

his hand to press the button and then stopped. The rest of the family followed his stare to the sign taped above the mailboxes. It said: No Pets—No Exceptions.

Erin, her arms wrapped tightly around the travel case, felt as if she were going to be sick.

Chapter Three

Mr. Lindsay recovered first.

"Erin, go back to the car," he ordered. "Quick now! Keep Rufus in his case, and roll down one window a little so you won't get too warm. I'll come out for you in a few minutes."

"But they won't let him live here!" Erin wailed. "It says so right there—'No Exceptions.' "

"Nonsense!" He grasped her shoulder and hustled her toward the door. "It's ridiculous to have a 'No Pets' rule in a place in this condition."

"If Rufus can't stay, I won't stay—" Erin began, but her father cut her short.

"We don't know yet whether any of us will be staying. We'll let this Mr. Grady show us around before we decide. Now go—and don't leave the car till I come for you."

In spite of the heat, Erin had goosebumps as she

hurried back across the street to the car. Her father didn't have to tell her to wait outside until he came; she'd *never* go inside that awful building if she didn't have to.

Still, the minutes passed slowly. Rufus seemed to know he was in trouble, and he whined piteously. Erin tried to comfort him, but she was too upset to be soothing. Ahead, the street stretched like a barren moonscape. Behind her, the view was the same, all the way to the big curve that had given them the first look at their apartment building. What would Heather and Meg and Emily think if they could see her now?

"Please don't be scared," she whispered to Rufus. "If you can't stay here, we'll run away together. We'll hitchhike back home."

Erin began to study the apartment building. It was six stories high, and many of the windows were empty. (Had some of the prisoners escaped from the castle?) Across the top of the building, every twenty feet or so, there was a smiling stone face. Long ago the faces had probably been beautiful, but rough Wisconsin winds had treated them badly. One had lost his (or her) nose.

Erin let her glance slide downward. The corner windows on the fourth floor were so different from all of the others that she wondered why she hadn't noticed them before. Swaths of pink net were looped back on either side like the curtains of a stage. From the edges of the draperies, bright-colored balls dangled and caught the light. What could they be? Erin shifted the travel case beside her and leaned over for a better look. Almost at once she ducked back. A round white face framed in ruffles was staring down at her.

Why didn't her father come back? A shadow fell across the street, and Erin looked up again, careful this time to keep her eyes away from those unusual fourth-floor windows and the watcher there. Clouds were piling up against the clear blue sky, and a distant rumble told her the weather was about to change. Rufus cried louder. He hated thunder. If he were at home, he'd be in the basement by now, curled up in the box the family called his storm cellar.

"It's okay, baby," Erin murmured. She tried shifting the travel case to the floor, but before she could do it, the front door of the apartment building opened and her father came out. He looked serious—worried, Erin decided—but as he crossed the street, his expression changed. He tilted his visored cap over one eye and leaned through the open car window.

"The coast is clear, sister," he said in a gangster whisper. "Drop my raincoat over the loot, and I'll smuggle it in."

Erin giggled in spite of herself. She helped her father arrange his raincoat over the travel case, and then she rolled up the windows and locked the car doors while he hurried across the street with the "loot." When she joined him in the foyer, he was fumbling with a key, trying to get through the inner door without turning Rufus upside down.

"I'll do it," Erin offered. A moment later they were in a long, dim hall, hot and drab but spotlessly clean.

"What happens if we get caught?" Erin whispered.

"We go into the dungeon for thirty years," her father said promptly. He must have been thinking about castles, too. "The fellow who manages the place is a real fussbudget. He knows the building will be torn down by next year this time, but he's not letting up one bit. It's his palace—and he doesn't want animals in it!"

Some palace! Erin thought. The hall smelled faintly of garlic, and there were big holes in the carpet. All of the doors remained firmly shut, but her father loped along on tiptoe, looking over his shoulder and rolling his eyes as if Mr. Grady, the fussbudget, might be lurking anywhere. It was a relief to get into the ancient elevator and close the door.

"Fifth floor, antique stoves and cats' pajamas," Mr. Lindsay intoned, switching from gangster to elevator operator. "Treasures for every taste." He grinned at Erin, and she realized he was trying hard to cheer her up.

Rufus chose that moment to let them know that he

was not cheered in the least. As the elevator trembled to a stop at the fifth floor, and the doors slid open, a throaty howl came from under the raincoat. The Lindsays looked at each other in panic.

"This way," Erin's father gasped, his face turning bright red. "Last apartment on the left." They raced along the hall, with Rufus shrieking more loudly at every step. As they reached number 508, the door flew open and Cowper leaned out.

Mr. Lindsay bounded through the opening, and Erin followed. "Good timing, Cowper, old man," Mr. Lindsay gasped. "How'd you know we were coming?"

Cowper gave him an incredulous look. "How could I *not* know?" he asked mildly. "It was either you guys or a herd of elephants."

Erin knelt and opened the cover of the travel case. "Poor baby," she crooned. "Were you scared?" She reached for the big cat, but he leaped away and streaked across the tiled entrance hall.

Straight ahead, an arch led into a living room. After a quick look, Rufus turned right and sped down a long hallway. Doors opened on either side, all the way to the end, where a tall chest of drawers covered most of the wall.

"Let him go," Mr. Lindsay advised. He was still puffing a little from their dash down the hall. "He's safe now, and he might as well get used to his new home. You too, Erin," he added. "Look around. Try it on for size."

So the decision had been made. They were staying. "Where's Mom?"

Mr. Lindsay pointed down the hall. "In one of the bedrooms, I think. Recovering from the kitchen."

A glance through the first door on the right told Erin why her mother had to "recover." The kitchen was crowded and narrow, with no windows, very different from the sparkling white and blue kitchen in Clinton. An ancient gas stove on high legs faced the door, next to a battered refrigerator. A small wooden table and three chairs stood against the end wall under an over-sized calendar.

The next door on the right was a closet, and the one after that led to the bathroom. On the other side were three bedrooms—a large one and two smaller ones, each with a single window. Erin found her mother in the last room, looking as if she'd just bitten into something sour.

"Cowper says he'll take this room if you don't want it," Mrs. Lindsay said. "It's the smallest, but he doesn't care. What do you think?"

Erin shrugged. "It doesn't matter." She edged around the narrow bed to look out the window. Just below the sill there was a ledge, about eighteen inches wide, that continued to the end of the building. The ledge cut off the view directly below, but beyond it the scene was as desolate and ugly from up here as it had been from the car.

Erin's mother came and stood beside her. "You're right, it's pretty dismal," she said as if Erin had spoken aloud. "But I think we can manage for a couple of months, don't you? The apartment *is* clean, and there's plenty of space. You'll have a room of your own to fix up any way you want to."

Erin sighed. "I guess so. What's that ledge for?"

"It's not for anything, as far as I can tell. Just a decoration. This building was put up a long, long time ago. They call an apartment like this a railroad flat because all the rooms open off a central 'aisle.' "

Together they went back to the middle bedroom. It was a little bigger than Cowper's room but not much. A studio couch stood along one wall, and there was a desk in front of the window. A dresser and a padded rocker completed the furnishings.

"Did you bring some posters from home?" Mrs. Lindsay asked. "They'd cheer things up a bit."

"A couple," Erin said. She didn't say so, but she doubted that her big pictures of kittens and bear cubs would help much. The room had a drab, sad look, as if no one had ever loved it.

Something brushed against Erin's leg. Rufus had returned and was looking up at her with a puzzled expression. Then he sprang past her to the windowsill and stared out.

"We'd better check all the screens," Mrs. Lindsay said. "We don't want him out on that ledge."

Horrified at the thought, Erin went from room to room, checking. She discovered that the ledge ended with the bedroom windows. From the living room you could look straight down to the patch of straggly lawn that ran along the side of the building.

"I think Ken Krueger must use only the front half of the apartment," her mother commented. "The living room, the kitchen, the bathroom, and the big bedroom. And he's certainly a saver," she added, looking with disapproval at the stacks of magazines piled under the living room end tables and in corners. "I'm going to pack up a lot of this stuff and put it away in boxes for the summer."

"Good thought," Mr. Lindsay agreed from the hall. He and Cowper had gone back to the car and were carrying in the first load of the Lindsays' belongings. "We've got our own stuff to clutter up the place." He pretended to totter under the weight of the suitcases he was carrying. "How about giving us a hand, Erin, my queen? The quicker we get the car emptied out, the quicker we can hit the road again and find the nearest pizza parlor."

Erin brightened. Pizza was a treat, even if it couldn't possibly be as good in Milwaukee as it was at Brown's

Pizza Parlor in Clinton. She followed her father and Cowper to the elevator, carefully closing the apartment door so that Rufus couldn't escape.

She felt better still when she'd carried her suitcase into the middle bedroom and opened it on the studio couch. Tucked among the clothes were some of the treasures she couldn't bear to leave behind for a whole summer. There was a snapshot of Heather and Emily; she propped that against a lamp on the dresser. There was the empty Joy perfume bottle Aunt Gina had given her, and there was the smiling baby raccoon, the smallest of her stuffed animals and the only one her mother would let her bring. The posters would come later. Just before they left home, the Lindsays had mailed two boxes of treasures to themselves at their new address.

"You can have my radio in here when it comes," Cowper said from the doorway. "Except on Thursdays. I'll need it Thursday nights." That was when piano recitals were scheduled on the public radio station.

"Thanks," Erin said and forced a smile. She knew the offer was his way of saying he was sorry he'd almost got Rufus killed. He never said things straight out.

"Pizza bus leaves in two minutes," Mr. Lindsay shouted from the kitchen. "Who wants to go?"

Erin went out into the hallway where Cowper was looking curiously at the chest of drawers that stood against the end wall.

"There's a door behind that thing," he said. "Mr. Grady, the superintendent, told us."

"Why would there be a door?" Erin could see no sign of one. "That's the back of the building, isn't it? There's no place else to go."

Cowper continued to look at the chest, almost as if he could see right through it. "Mr. Grady said at first they were going to build little porches out there for all the rear apartments. But before the wrought-iron railings were delivered, the builders ran out of money. So they just sealed up the doors and forgot about the porches."

"That's crazy," Erin declared. She turned and started toward the living room, determined to ask her parents if Cowper was making up a lie.

"There really is a door," Cowper insisted, trailing behind her. "It just won't get you anywhere."

"Figures," Erin replied grumpily. "It just won't get you anywhere" fitted this entire summer, as far as she was concerned.

Chapter Four

"I'm going to be late," Cowper groaned. He pushed away his half-eaten cereal. "I know it."

"No, you're not," Mrs. Lindsay said. "You have plenty of time, Cowper. The class doesn't begin until nine thirty, you know."

"But we don't even know where the conservatory is." Erin thought her foster brother sounded as if he were going to cry, which would be very strange. She'd never seen him cry, even when his mother and father were killed. "He isn't a weeper," Mr. Lindsay had said. "Some people aren't."

Erin wondered if that was true, or if Cowper just didn't care as much as most people. She was a crier, herself; sad books, sad movies, any story about a mistreated animal—they all brought tears to her eyes.

"We could have a flat tire," Cowper persisted, "or get lost—or run out of gas!"

Mr. Lindsay squeezed a last spoonful of juice from his grapefruit and stood up. He saluted and tried to click his heels together—a wasted effort since he was wearing sneakers and they didn't click.

"We who are about to try, salute you," he bellowed, and then he winked at Cowper. "Fear not! We shall accomplish this mission." He marched out of the kitchen, and Cowper followed, looking unconvinced. Mrs. Lindsay went after them, and Erin was left alone. All alone. *Don't be a droop*, she told herself sternly, but it didn't help much. The bad time was beginning—a summer of excitement or a summer of nothing, depending on whether you were a genius or not.

Maybe today was worse because yesterday hadn't been too bad. Erin and her mother had found a supermarket four blocks away and had filled the refrigerator and cupboards with supplies. In the afternoon Erin and Cowper had watched TV—there were a couple of channels they couldn't get in Clinton—and Mrs. Lindsay had baked Erin's favorite cake (yellow, with fudge frosting). Erin had tried to pretend that this was the way their time in Milwaukee was going to be—the family doing things together—but she knew she was the only one who wanted that. The others were just waiting for their real summer to begin.

Mrs. Lindsay reappeared at the kitchen door. "Come on, Erin," she said enthusiastically. "Let's take Cowper to his class the first day. Dad and I will probably have to take turns once our summer school classes start, so we all should know how to find the conservatory."

"Not me," Erin said. "I don't have to know." She took another bite of her half-eaten toast. "I'll be okay here."

"Erin!" Her mother sounded exasperated. "Please don't be difficult. This is a good chance for you to see more of the city. It's really very beautiful, once you get away from this section."

"I'll see it some other time," Erin said. "I want to—to write a letter to Heather."

"I am going to be late. I know it!" That was Cowper in the hall, sounding more panicky than ever.

Mrs. Lindsay looked over her shoulder. "Then promise you won't let anyone in while we're gone," she said. "You know, Dad and I are going to try to arrange our classes so you'll never be alone here for more than a few minutes."

"What could happen?" Erin scoffed. "I stay alone in Clinton sometimes."

"Alone is one thing," her mother retorted. "Lonely is something else. It's easy to feel lonely in an unfamiliar place."

She was right. As soon as the door closed behind them, Erin began to wish she'd gone along. The stillness thudded in her ears, and the string of empty rooms made her think of prison cells. Rufus followed her down the hall, his ears laid back, his eyes huge, as if he suspected danger at every doorway. When Erin tried to pick him up, he darted away and hid behind the studio couch in her bedroom.

Writing to Heather proved impossible. Erin took out her box of stationery, but when she started to write, thinking about home and friends made her more miserable than ever. *Did you see a ghost at the schoolhouse?* She stared at the words and then crumpled up the paper. It would break her heart if the answer was yes.

After a while she wandered back to the kitchen, where the breakfast dishes waited. Sara Crewe would wash them. *Well, why not?* she thought, yawning. Cleaning up the kitchen might be the most thrilling thing she did all day.

She told Heather about it in a letter a couple of days later. Not that washing Ken Krueger's faded china turned out to be fun. Not that she especially enjoyed stacking plates and cereal bowls in the tall, narrow cabinet or wiping down the table or scrubbing the scarred sink. But taking out the garbage was something else.

Taking out the garbage had been an adventure.

The incinerator chute was at the end of the fifth-floor hallway near the stairwell that ran all the way down to the first floor. Erin thought the chute was the most

interesting thing—maybe the only interesting thing—
in the apartment building. You opened a little door,
dropped in the bag of garbage, and somewhere far below (*in the castle dungeon!*) fires raged, swallowing up
whatever hurtled down. Erin tried to imagine the goblin who tended the fire. At night he probably slept in
one of the dungeons. He hadn't seen the sun in years.

Erin opened the chute and listened briefly before
tossing the garbage bag into the opening. It was very
quiet down there. She leaned forward and whistled
through her teeth, but there was no answering whistle
from below. Of course there wasn't! Embarrassed, she
let the little door swing shut and looked around hastily
to see if anyone was watching. She was just in time to
see something orange-red and furry dart past her and
down the stairs.

"Rufus!"

With a squeal of anguish Erin raced after her cat.
She'd left the apartment door open just a crack so that
she could get back in, forgetting that Rufus considered
every partly open door a challenge. Now he was running loose in this terrible place where he wasn't wanted.

What would happen if Mr. Grady saw him? The
Lindsays would probably be ordered out of their apartment, and her mother and father and Cowper would
think she'd made it happen on purpose. As Erin dashed
down the stairs, she thought of an even more chilling

possibility. If Mr. Grady caught Rufus, he might take him prisoner and do something horrible to him. *And it'll be all my fault. . . . No, it'll be Cowbird's fault. Again! We wouldn't be here if it weren't for his dumb old master class.*

When Erin reached the fourth floor, Rufus was halfway down the hall, moving fast. She started after him, not daring to call. And then the real nightmare began. A door opened almost in front of her, and a tall thin man stepped out. He was wearing blue jeans and a T-shirt, and he had a huge ring of keys fastened to a loop of his belt. *Keys to the dungeon!* In one hand he carried a wrench, in the other a plunger. He was talking over his shoulder to someone in the apartment, and his back was to Rufus.

He stopped talking to throw out a long arm and halt Erin's headlong charge.

"No running in the halls, young lady!" He spoke in a kind of growl. "Who might you be, anyways?"

"Erin—Erin Lindsay." She backed away from him. "I-I live on the fifth floor—just for the summer."

"Oh, you're one of them." He eyed her as if she were an alien from another world. "Well, I guess I didn't say nothing to your folks about running in the halls. Didn't think I had to. That boy looks like he knows how to behave himself. Can't see why a big girl like you . . ."

Erin's face burned. She couldn't tell this ogre she'd been chasing her cat.

"I say a big girl like you should know better. We have old people living here. You could bowl 'em right over. Next thing you know, they'd be suing the management."

Thirty feet down the hall, Rufus had stopped and was looking over his shoulder. Erin trembled. What if he decided to come back to see what was going on?

"I was l-looking for something I lost," she stammered. "I dropped it when we were moving in," she added, turning the truth into a lie.

"Well, I don't see why you expect to find it on the fourth floor since you're up on five," Mr. Grady growled. "I can tell you right now, girly, you won't find anything lying around in these halls. I sweep 'em every day of my life. Sundays, too."

Another door opened, this one just a little beyond where Rufus crouched. A woman stepped out—or maybe it was a girl. In the dim light Erin couldn't be sure. For what seemed an endless moment they all stood there, Erin and Mr. Grady, Rufus and the stranger. Then the newcomer bent down and scooped up the cat. With one swift move she dropped him into her shopping bag and straightened, just as Mr. Grady turned around and glared at her.

"Good morning, Mr. Grady. It's a lovely day, isn't it?" The voice was light, girlish, full of laughter.

"Morning." The superintendent looked as if he'd like to say it wasn't a lovely day at all. "Just remember,

no running in the halls," he snapped turning back to
Erin. "Knock somebody down. Lawsuit. Always blame
the super. That's the way people are." Muttering under
his breath, he stomped past her and down the stairs.

Erin waited till he was out of sight, then scooted
down the hall. "Oh, thank you!" she exclaimed.
"Thanks for saving my cat's life." At the sound of her
voice, Rufus's head popped up from the canvas bag. He
enjoyed empty bags and boxes as much as he liked
partly opened doors.

His rescuer smiled. "I didn't, really," she said. "But
Mr. Grady would have been very angry. And he certainly would have made you get rid of your pet. He's a
bear about rules."

The woman was tiny, hardly as tall as Erin, and very
thin. Narrow white sausage curls framed her face, and
there were explosions of tiny wrinkles around her eyes,
as if the force of her bright blue gaze had left its mark.
She must be very old, Erin thought, but then she wasn't
so sure. The woman's hair and her wrinkles made her
look old, but her voice and her eyes were young.

Erin knelt and lifted Rufus from the bag. "Poor
baby," she crooned.

"You'd better come inside for a few minutes," the
woman suggested. "Give the bear time to get back to
his den. You wouldn't want to run into him again, I'm
sure."

Erin shuddered. Now that she'd met Mr. Grady, she was going to be more careful than ever to keep Rufus hidden.

"You just sit in here and rest a minute, dear," the sweet voice coaxed. "I was going shopping, but it can wait. My name is Molly Panca. What's yours?"

"Erin Lindsay."

"And my friend in the bag? I can't keep calling him the cat."

"Rufus Lindsay."

They were in a tiny living room, not half the size of the Lindsays'. A kitchen opened off one side; the second door was closed. The living room windows were the ones Erin had seen from the car two days ago. The pink net curtains were held back with strings of artificial roses. Tiny silver and gold Christmas balls hung from the crocheted hems and sparkled in the sun.

The rest of the room was just as unusual. Pastel pink shawls covered the couch and the two chairs, and there were artificial flowers everywhere. Bright bouquets stood on the end tables, the bookcase, and in a basket in one corner. A string of silk daisies was wound around a lampshade. The air was heavy and sweet.

"Would you like a glass of iced tea, dear? There's nothing as refreshing as iced tea on a summer's day."

"No, thank you." Erin suddenly remembered that her apartment door was still standing open. "I'll have to go back upstairs—soon as I'm sure that man is gone."

Rufus slithered off her lap and stared up at Molly Panca. His look said he'd never seen anyone like her.

"That's a pretty skirt," Erin said shyly. She remembered one like it from a family photo album, a picture of her grandmother when she was in high school. The skirt was cut from pink felt, and a white felt poodle with a sequin collar danced along the hem. With it, Molly Panca wore a long-sleeved blouse with a ruffled collar. Her sneakers had pink laces.

"I bought this skirt at the Goodwill," Molly said proudly. "I only paid fifty cents for it—can you believe that?" She looked kindly at Erin's jeans and T-shirt. "Do you shop at the Goodwill store, too?"

"I don't even know where the Goodwill store is," Erin said. "We just moved here the day before yesterday. From Clinton. We're going back at the end of August." It sounded a long way off.

"So right now you're lonesome," Molly Panca commented, as if Erin had said that, too. "And Rufus is lonesome. This summer will be harder on him than it will be on you. People can make their own magic."

Erin squirmed uncomfortably. Molly Panca sounded like a mind reader who didn't particularly agree with what she was discovering in Erin's head. "I'd better go home now. I left our door open. And besides, my mom and dad will be back pretty soon. They were just taking my brother to his class."

Her hostess beamed. "You have a brother? Well, you are lucky, aren't you? I always wanted a brother when I was your age."

Erin bit her lip.

"I hope you'll come back to see me again soon," Molly Panca continued. "My family would love to meet you. Pop Rufus in a sack and bring him along if you want to. He'd enjoy a change, I'm sure."

She reached into her shopping bag and brought out a shabby green wallet. "Here's my card," she said grandly. "You tell your mother and father I'm here if they ever need me. I love to help my neighbors—no charge, of course."

With her arms full of Rufus, Erin couldn't hold the card high enough to read it. Besides, she was in a hurry to leave. In another minute Molly Panca might ask why the Lindsays were in Milwaukee and what kind of class Cowper was taking. And then she'd tell Erin again how lucky she was to have a brother.

"Thanks again for saving Rufus," Erin said. "I—we really appreciate it."

Molly Panca smiled with dazzling sweetness. "My pleasure, dear." She gave Rufus a farewell scratch behind the ears. "Come again, old fellow. We do enjoy company."

Back upstairs, Erin was relieved to find that her parents hadn't returned. They would be annoyed if they knew she'd gone out and left the door open. She went into the living room and curled up in an overstuffed chair to examine Molly Panca's card.

MOLLY ELIZABETH PANCA it said in fine black script. Under that was a single word: *Medium*. A third line read *Seance by appointment*.

Medium? Wasn't a medium a person who talked to dead people?

Even though the living room was stuffy-hot, Erin shivered with pleasure. Here at last was something neat she could tell Heather and Emily and Meg. Meeting a medium was almost as exciting as exploring a haunted schoolhouse. Erin shivered again, wondering what Molly Panca had meant when she talked about her family? Her apartment had been very small, very quiet. Erin didn't see how there could be people in the other rooms.

Not *live* people, anyway.

Chapter Five

"A medium." Mr. Lindsay fingered Molly Panca's card and grinned at Erin. "Some people have all the luck. Imagine meeting a medium on your second morning in the big city."

"But I can hardly believe you went into the apartment of a total stranger." Erin's mother sounded distracted. She had a stack of catalogs and forms spread out on the coffee table and was busy lining up the classes she wanted to take this summer.

Erin frowned. "She saved Rufus's life, Mom. Did you want me to say, 'No, my mother won't let me talk to you'?"

Mr. Lindsay laid the card on the table. "A bit testy, aren't we?" he said mildly. "Your mother just wants to keep you out of trouble, my queen."

"But you always tell me to be polite. And now you say—"

"That's enough." Mrs. Lindsay pushed aside the pamphlet. "Of course we want you to be polite. But we don't know this person, and she does sound rather—peculiar."

"Maybe she's crazy," Cowper said. He was at the far end of the couch, sitting cross-legged, an anxious, almost angry expression on his face.

"She's not crazy," Erin said hotly. "She's a really nice person, and she's my friend."

"You only met her today," Cowper argued. "She can't be your friend. Friends take a long time."

Erin gritted her teeth. He was right, of course; Molly Panca wasn't her friend the way Heather and Meg and Emily were her friends. But Molly wasn't crazy, either. She was just different.

"You'd have to be crazy to think you could talk to dead people, wouldn't you?" Cowper wondered. "You'd have to be off the wall."

"Liar!" Furious, Erin jumped up and stormed down the hall to her bedroom. It was drab and depressing in there, but at least she didn't have to listen to her foster brother.

Erin's father knocked and came in, a few minutes later. "You mustn't let Cowper get to you," he said. "The poor kid's kind of upset, and he has to take it out on someone. He thinks he's not going to be able to keep up with the rest of the people in his class."

"Why not?" Erin was surprised. She hadn't known Cowbird *ever* had any doubts about how good he was.

Mr. Lindsay shrugged. "The other students are all adults. He says they've had more training in harmony, more—oh, I don't know. It's all Greek to me. Anyway, he's scared, and that's why he's grumpy."

So for once maybe Cowbird wasn't going to be his teacher's shining star. Erin tried to feel sorry for him, but it wasn't easy.

"Anyway, I'm sure the boy's wrong about how well he's going to do," Mr. Lindsay continued. "Your mother talked to the instructor for a minute or two, and he was very excited about having Cowper in the class. But you know Cowper—once he gets an idea you can't shake him. Anyway," he hurried on, "I came in here for two reasons, madam. Number one, how would you like it if I brought home some books for you from the university library? There are probably lots of good books for kids."

Erin nodded eagerly. "Ghost stories! Suspense!"

"Right. And other good stuff, too. Second," her father continued, "you'll be happy to hear that the boxes from home just arrived. Your mother said you packed some posters and stuff."

"And my skateboard," Erin said. The arrival of the boxes *was* good news. In Clinton, skateboarding had been her favorite activity, next to reading and watching

mysteries on television. Whenever she was especially
angry with Cowbird, she'd snatch up her board and the
bag that held her shoes, helmet, and knee pads and
hurry off to Market Park. A half hour of practicing G
turns and Ollies, of roaring up the ramp and pulling air
at the top before she swooped down again—that was
the best medicine for the raging resentment that sometimes made her head ache and set her stomach churning. She was good at skateboarding. It was something
Cowbird had never even tried; he might hurt his hands.

She followed her father down the hall to where two
big cartons were waiting in the foyer. Her mother was
on her knees between them.

"Might as well leave them here while we unpack,"
she said without looking up. "I believe there's something for every room in the apartment." She lifted out
a long cardboard mailing tube that had been stretched
diagonally across the top of one box. "Here are your
posters, Erin. Just what you've been waiting for."

Erin took the tube and propped it against the wall.
There were layers of towels and bed linens in the box,
a handful of her mother's favorite kitchen tools, the
camcorder, a dictionary, and finally, at the very bottom, her skateboard. Erin lifted it out, admiring for
the hundredth time the bright decals on the underside.
Her knee and wrist protectors were tucked into corners
of the box, and her helmet was stuffed full of wash-
cloths and dish towels.

She ran her fingertips over the slick surface of the board. For a moment the fresh green smell of Market Park was all around her, so real that she ached with longing.

Cowper had come out into the hall and was lifting his radio from the other carton. His eyes were solemn behind his glasses as he watched Erin check her board.

"You won't be able to use that here," he said. "The sidewalk's a mess."

"I will too," Erin snapped. Then she remembered what her father had said, and she lowered her voice. "I don't care about a few little bumps."

"They aren't *little* bumps," Cowper said. "Whole squares of concrete are missing. And there's lots of holes. You'll break a leg or something."

"I will *not*. Just because you're afraid—"

"Erin, Cowper, stop it!" Mrs. Lindsay rocked back on her heels and wiped her forehead. "Do you have to argue about every little thing?"

Erin gathered her helmet and other equipment and stood up, clutching the skateboard. "I'm going outside," she said coldly. "Right now."

"You watch it, now," her father called after her. "Cowper's right about that sidewalk. It's a disaster. I guess the city fathers figure there's no point in fixing it if the whole area's going to be turned into an expressway in the next couple of years."

Erin scowled. Cowbird couldn't stand up on a board

for ten seconds, and if he ever tried a simple G turn he'd fall flat on his face. Yet if *he* said the sidewalk was too rough for skateboarding, everybody agreed with him.

Everybody but me. Erin slammed the door behind her, much harder than necessary.

The day was steamy when Erin stepped out onto the wide front steps. It was the first time she'd been outside since she'd driven with her mother to buy groceries yesterday morning. Then she'd been wondering where they would find a grocery store in this clutter of empty lots and crumbling foundations. She hadn't even glanced at the sidewalk in front of the apartment. Now she realized that Cowper and her father were right. As far as she could see in either direction the sidewalk was ruined. Whole sections were gone, and what was left was uneven and full of holes. No one, not even the skateboard champion of the universe, could skate on that!

Erin leaned against one of the stone lions that guarded the door, and her anger seeped away. Despair took its place. If she couldn't skateboard during the long days ahead, what could she do?

An old man—the same one they'd seen the day they arrived—came out of the building dragging his grocery cart behind him over the bumpy sidewalk. A few minutes later, two elderly ladies pushed open the door and stared at Erin before continuing down the steps. *Must be going to the grocery store*, she thought. She watched the women pick their way cautiously over the broken pavement, holding onto each other's arms for support. They had a long walk ahead of them on a hot day.

I feel sorry for them, Erin thought and was momentarily pleased to have had a good Sara Crewe–like feeling without working at it. *But I feel sorrier for me*, she added, and of course that wasn't like Sara Crewe at all.

Cars and trucks moved up and down Kirby Avenue. A van full of children rolled by, and a little girl waved and smiled from the back window. Erin waved back, but she didn't smile. She couldn't. She felt as if the world were winding down and might end at any minute.

"If you're going to just sit here, you might as well scratch behind my left ear. It's been itching for years."

The voice was thin, whiny, and so close that Erin jumped. She stared unbelievingly into the eyes of the stone lion.

"Don't gape," the lion whined. "People always gape, and it makes me nervous."

Erin thought she must be dreaming. The stone lips didn't move, and the eyes didn't blink, but the lion was talking, as sure as he crouched there.

Chapter Six

"It talked!" Erin had waited till the rippling sounds of a piano told her Cowper was busy with the Thursday night radio concert. Now she faced her mother and father with the incredible news. "It was a miracle!"

Mrs. Lindsay smiled, and Mr. Lindsay slapped his forehead in mock astonishment. "What did he say?" he demanded. "That he was tired of just lion around?"

Erin ignored the pun. "He said, 'Scratch me behind the left ear. It's been itching for years.' "

Her mother and father burst out laughing. "And did you scratch him?" Mr. Lindsay wanted to know.

Erin frowned. "I ran back inside." She knew what had happened was hard to believe, but she didn't want her parents to laugh. "You'd have run, too, if you'd heard him."

"Erin, you have a wonderful sense of humor," Mrs. Lindsay said. "I was beginning to think you'd lost it someplace between here and Clinton. Obviously not."

"And a great imagination," her father added. "I've often wondered what a statue would say if it could talk. Now I know."

"I'm not making this up!" Erin exclaimed. "The lion talked to me."

Her mother's smile began to slip away. "All right," she said, "don't carry the joke too far. A funny story is one thing but—"

"If Cowper told you the lion talked, I bet you'd go right downstairs and listen for yourself. But when I tell you, you say I'm lying."

Mr. Lindsay stood up and stretched. "I'm game," he said. "If I thought he'd talk to me, I'd sit on the steps all day and all night."

Erin saw the little grin that tugged at the corners of his mouth. "Don't bother," she said with as much dignity as she could manage. "It doesn't matter whether you believe me or not."

But of course it did matter. Over the next few days, when her parents went to their classes at the university and Cowper was delivered each morning to the conservatory, Erin thought about the lion a lot.

She tried to describe her adventure in a letter to Heather. *I was sitting there by myself, and all of a sudden* . . . She started again. *The scariest thing happened to me yesterday.* . . .

It was no use. Heather might not laugh at her the way her parents had, but she wouldn't believe what had happened either. She and Meg and Emily had probably had such a thrilling time investigating the haunted schoolhouse that they weren't giving Erin Lindsay a thought.

The next few days dragged by. Erin listened to soaps and read two suspense novels her father brought home from the university library. Sometimes she sat on the front steps of the apartment building, wishing she had a friend to talk to but finding no one. The people who went up and down the wide steps were all old and worried-looking. Few of them bothered to say hello.

Sara Crewe would find something exciting to do, she told herself. And still she sat there.

Once, when she was sure no one was looking, she reached up and scratched the lion behind his left ear. He didn't even purr. By the fourth day, she began to wonder, just a little, if her mother and father might be right. Maybe the lion's voice really had been in her imagination. Sara Crewe always made up fantastical stories to cheer herself when she was depressed. Was it possible to do that without even knowing it?

On the fifth morning, after Erin's mother had left with Cowper and her father had gone to their bedroom to study, Erin decided to give the lion one more chance. She hung the apartment key on a string around her neck and let herself out, closing the door softly behind her.

It was a dark, overcast day, so the long hallway was even drearier than usual. Erin turned to the back stairway, deciding she'd rather walk than ride in the creaking elevator. On the fourth-floor landing she stopped, then started down the hall toward Molly Panca's apartment. Maybe Molly would listen to her story of the talking lion without laughing; after all, a medium should be used to strange happenings.

"*Help!*"

Erin jumped as the harsh cry broke the silence of the hallway. The voice came from apartment 405, just a few feet from where she was standing. Erin looked around, hoping someone else had heard it, but all the doors remained tightly closed.

"*Help!*" The cry came again, followed by another, even more startling. "*Save the poor sailor!*"

Hesitantly, Erin turned the doorknob of 405. If the door was locked, she'd have to run upstairs and get her father. But it swung open easily, and she found herself staring into a living room the size of Molly Panca's. An old man lay on the couch that filled one wall, his head pillowed on his arm. A large green parrot perched on the arm of the couch at his feet.

"*Help the poor sailor!*" the parrot squawked. He swiveled his head to peer into the kitchen where flames leaped from a frying pan on the stove.

Erin hurtled across the living room and into the

kitchen. The fire was licking at the bottoms of the cupboards above the stove and had already blackened one wall. A dish towel on the counter was starting to smolder.

She looked around desperately for something she could use to smother the fire. On the tiny kitchen table was a baking sheet covered with neat circles of dough waiting to be fried. Erin snatched it up and slid it over the flaming skillet with enough force to send the doughnuts flying in every direction.

Something heavy landed on her shoulder. Sharp claws dug through her T-shirt. "Good girl!" the parrot cheered. He hung on fiercely while Erin turned off the gas burner and dropped the scorched dish towel into the sink. Then he flapped to the counter and paced its length with a haughty expression.

"What's all this now?" a voice demanded. Erin whirled around and discovered the old man standing close behind her. His white hair stood up in tufts all over his head, and his glasses rode on the tip of his nose. He looked frightened and angry.

"Who let you in?" he demanded. "What're you do- ing to my poor Sailor?" He held out an arm, and the parrot promptly strolled up to his shoulder.

Erin pointed at the blackened back wall. "Your par- rot called for help," she explained. "I was walking down the hall and—"

"Good gravy!" The man ran gnarled fingers through his hair, making it stand up straighter than ever. "The doughnuts! I remember now. Got 'em all ready to fry, and then I thought I'd rest a little while the oil was heating. . . . Don't ever do that!" he turned on Erin severely. "When you're heating oil you better be on your toes every minute, and don't you forget it!"

Erin nodded. "I-I don't make doughnuts," she said. "My mother says it's too dangerous."

"Your mother's a smart woman," the old man said. He touched the charred wall and shook his head. "I'll have to fix this up," he said. "Don't want Grady to see it, that's for sure. Have enough trouble with him over Sailor here. The man don't like pets, you know." He picked up a limp ring of dough from the floor. "Wasn't really my fault, anyway. My wife said, 'Cook,' so I cooked. I bet she's sorry now."

Erin looked around. There was nothing about the stark little kitchen to suggest a woman worked there, but she was relieved to hear the old man had a wife to look after him. In spite of his blustering, Erin could tell he was deeply upset.

"When your wife comes home," she said, "please tell her I'm sorry about the doughnuts. I couldn't see anything to smother the fire with except the baking sheet."

"Oh, she's here right now," the man said cheerfully. "Can't talk to her, of course, but she's here. Been dead six years this August, but she never leaves me—not for a minute."

"Really?" Erin backed across the living room, ready to run. "I have to go now," she said nervously. "You'll be okay, won't you?"

"Of course I'll be okay. Sailor and me—we do just fine." He put out a hand. "Name's Barnhart. What's yours?"

Erin told him her name and explained that she had just moved in for the summer. "I'm glad to meet you—and Sailor." She reached for the door.

"Poor Sailor," the parrot commented. He twisted his head to look again at the mess in the kitchen. Then he turned back to Erin. "Good girl," he announced firmly.

"Just don't try to make doughnuts," Mr. Barnhart said. "Better stick to meat loaf."

Erin let herself out and closed the door behind her. Laughter bubbled up inside her. She'd probably saved Mr. Barnhart's life, and all she'd gotten for her trouble was a warning. Except for Sailor, of course, she corrected herself with a giggle. Sailor thought she was great.

The laughter faded as she imagined herself telling her mother and father and Cowper about this new adventure. Her mother would be appalled at the danger. Her father would say, "First a talking stone lion, then a ghost in the kitchen. What goes on here?"

Too bad I didn't have the camcorder with me, she thought. *Erin Lindsay, Girl Firefighter.* It would have been fun to show that to her friends when she got home.

Erin stopped short, the word *camcorder* ringing in her ears. Camcorder—what exciting thing could she do with the camcorder? Suddenly, she knew.

Sara Crewe would be proud of my new idea, she thought gleefully. She went skipping down the hall without a thought of what the ogre Mr. Grady might do if he caught her.

Chapter Seven

"First a talking stone lion, then a ghost in a kitchen! What goes on here?" Mr. Lindsay raised his eyebrows at Erin over the top of the sports page. "Do you s'pose it has something to do with your friend the medium? What's her name—Molly Hanky-Panky? Maybe the spirits sort of hang around this building because she has the welcome sign out."

"Her name is Molly Panca," Erin said. "And I'm only telling you what happened. Mr. Barnhart *said* his wife was right there in the kitchen with us."

"Well, whatever," her mother interrupted, "I'm very proud of you, Erin. Some people your age wouldn't have had the least idea what to do in that kind of emergency. Would you know what to do, Cowper?"

Cowper frowned. "I wouldn't have thrown all those doughnuts around," he said. "I like doughnuts. Why not just dump some water on the fire?"

Erin shook her head disgustedly. "If you did that, you'd burn down the whole building!" she exclaimed. "You can't put out an oil fire with water. The water just splashes the oil around. You have to cut off the oxygen with a cover. Or you can throw flour on a fire," she added digging deeper into her memory. Last summer she and Heather and Meg had gone on a weekend camp-out sponsored by the Clinton Recreation Department. The camp counselor had taught them a lot about fires and outdoor cooking.

"Oh well." Cowper shrugged as if the whole question was unimportant. But he looked impressed in spite of himself.

"Anyway," Erin said, "I have something very important to tell you. And everybody has to listen"—she looked sternly at Cowper— "because this *affects* you."

"Wow!" Erin's father raised his hands, palms forward, on either side of his head. "I'm all ears, ma'am."

"I—Erin Lindsay—am going to make a video! A mystery-ghost-story video!"

Silence. "Well," Mrs. Lindsay said uncertainly, "that sounds like quite a project, dear."

"How?" Cowper demanded. "How can you do that?"

Erin could hardly wait to explain. "First I'm going to write the script, and it's going to be really scary. And then I'm going to direct it. And film it with the camcorder."

"Direct who?" Cowper asked suspiciously. "Film who?"

Erin grinned. "You," she announced. "And Mom and Dad. And me. We're all going to be in it."

"Don't look at me," Cowper said. "I don't know how to act."

"I'll show you." Erin had made up her mind not to let anyone discourage her. "The whole thing—the acting I mean—will probably just take an hour or so. And I'll give you an easy part. Maybe you can be the dead body."

"Oh, Erin!" Her mother and father exchanged glances. "I'm sure Cowper can do something more than play dead. We'll all help. You just tell us what to do."

"I want a *big* part," Mr. Lindsay announced. "I've always thought I'd make a better actor than a schoolteacher."

Erin nodded happily. It had been easier than she'd expected. Cowbird would probably be stubborn, but this once—she fought down a surge of anger—this once he was going to have to do what she wanted.

That night Erin didn't fall asleep for a long time. At first, ideas for her movie crowded into her head. Then she began to think about her father's suggestion that spirits hung around the apartment building because they felt welcome there. He'd been teasing, of course; still, Erin certainly had had some odd experiences since she'd come to Milwaukee. Tomorrow, she decided, she'd pay Molly Panca a visit and find out what a medium did.

In the morning, however, all of her plans were postponed. At breakfast her mother and father announced that, since neither of them had classes that afternoon, they'd decided it was time for a family outing.

"We're going to the zoo?" Erin said slowly, hardly daring to believe.

"We'll have a quick lunch as soon as Dad and Cowper get home from the conservatory," Mrs. Lindsay said, her eyes sparkling. "Or—this is even better— we'll pack a lunch and take it with us! I've been to the Milwaukee Zoo, and it's wonderful."

Erin was thrilled. "I'm going to take notes for my career notebook," she said. "A zookeeper is my fourth favorite thing to be when I grow up, if I'm not a veterinarian or an actress or a ghost-detective."

Cowper took a drink of milk. "You have to get straight A's to be a veterinarian," he said through a milky mustache. "I heard a man talk about it on the radio."

"So?" Erin glared at him. "Starting next year I'm going to get straight A's. I can if I try."

She glanced at her mother and saw a flicker of doubt, quickly covered with a smile. "Well, you certainly can do better than you have in the last couple of years,"

Mrs. Lindsay said. "But straight A's aren't the most important thing in the world. You must just do the best you can."

Erin's face grew hot. Her mother didn't believe she could be terrific if she made up her mind to be and worked hard at it. Her mother only believed in geniuses. And that wasn't fair, because genius was something you were born with, like blue eyes or red hair. You didn't have to work hard to become a genius.

For a while after Cowper and her father left, Erin stayed in her room, reading and cuddling Rufus. Gradually, as she thought about the afternoon ahead, her spirits lifted. The zoo would be great, and when they came home, she'd start working on her video script. She already had a couple of good ideas.

At eleven she changed into her red shorts and Save the Whales T-shirt and wandered out to the kitchen, where her mother was making sandwiches.

"Cream cheese and cucumber for me, cheddar with sliced pickles for you, bologna and mustard for your father, and peanut butter with banana for Cowper." Mrs. Lindsay dropped another packet of sandwiches into the picnic basket. "Also, peaches and apples, chips, cookies, a Thermos of lemonade and a six-pack of soda. Am I forgetting anything?"

Erin shook her head. "I'm glad we're going to the zoo," she said dreamily. "It'll be fun."

Mrs. Lindsay laid paper napkins on top of the lunch and covered the basket with a towel. "I'm glad, too," she said. "We haven't done anything together for ages." She gave Erin a quick pat on the head. "I like your movie project, dear. We can all have fun with that."

Erin munched a potato chip. "Not Cowper," she said. "He doesn't like anything I like."

Mrs. Lindsay stopped wiping the table and gave Erin a long look. "You're wrong about that," she said. "Completely wrong. Can't you see how much he admires you? He may not say so, but it's obvious to me. It's just that music is his one great interest, and that has to come first."

Erin sighed. "I wish—" she began. "I wish—"

"You wish what?"

She couldn't say the words. *I wish things could be the way they used to be—before Cowper.* Sara Crewe would never say those words. She wouldn't even think them. *But I can't help wishing. Why couldn't Cowper be somebody else's genius?*

Erin wished it more than ever five minutes later, when the door opened and Cowper and her father came in. Her father's expression was somber, and Cowper was wearing what Erin privately called The Look. His jaw was clenched and he stared at the floor.

"We're all set," Mrs. Lindsay told them gaily. "Cowper, change into your shorts, and we'll be on our way."

Oh no, we won't, Erin thought. Her heart sank as she looked from her father to her foster brother.

"I'm afraid we have a change in plans here, folks." Mr. Lindsay tried to sound offhand. "Mr. Salzman— he's the man who's conducting the master class, Erin— Mr. Salzman has invited some people from the university's music department to hear Cowper play to- morrow. There's a chance—just a chance—that he'll be asked to make a guest appearance at one of the univer- sity's summer concerts."

Mrs. Lindsay's stricken expression changed to a broad smile. "Why, that's wonderful!" She bent and hugged Cowper, who continued to stare at the floor.

"What's that got to do with going to the zoo?" Erin demanded. "What do you mean about changing plans?"

Cowper looked up for the first time. "I have to prac- tice this afternoon," he said flatly.

"But you practice all the time!" Erin exclaimed. "You practice for hours and hours and—"

"Cowper's concerned about being at his best for the audition," Mr. Lindsay explained. "He wants to go to the zoo as much as you do, Erin, but—"

"Oh no, he doesn't!" Suddenly, Erin was angrier than she'd ever been in her life. "He doesn't care any- thing about the zoo. And he doesn't care about how much I want to go. Mom wants to go, too. And she has the lunch all packed. He doesn't care about anything but himself!"

Cowper took a startled step backward, and Mrs. Lindsay put a hand on Erin's shoulder. "There has to be some way we can work this out," Mrs. Lindsay said. "Maybe we can have our picnic lunch here, and then we'll take you back to the conservatory for an hour or so, Cowper, and then . . ." Her voice trailed off as Mr. Lindsay shook his head.

"The zoo's way on the other side of town," he said. "There's no point in going there if we're just going to have part of an afternoon to look around. Better to save it for another day when we'll all have lots of time."

"That's not fair!" Erin cried. She turned on her foster brother furiously. "You're doing this on purpose. You know I want to go, so you've decided to spoil it. And you're going to let him," she shouted at her parents. "No matter what he wants, it's fine with you!"

"Erin, stop!" Mrs. Lindsay looked stunned. "You know that isn't true. We love you both, and we try to do what's right for both of you. In this case"—she looked anxiously at Cowper—"if you're certain you need extra practice before the audition, Cowper, then of course you must do it. You can't pass up this opportunity. We can go to the zoo another day, and we will."

"Sure we will," Mr. Lindsay said heartily. "Just

think how proud you'll be if Cowper's invited to play at a university concert, Erin. How many nine-year-olds does that ever happen to? There'll be pictures in the paper—the works! Who knows what might happen next?"

If he'd been trying, he couldn't have made Erin feel worse. Leaving Clinton for the whole summer had been bad enough; still, Erin had been trying to make the best of it. But if Cowbird became famous now, every summer would probably be like this one. They'd wander all over the country, from one concert to another. Erin would never have a chance to do what she wanted to do.

A hard knot formed in her throat. "I know what'll happen next!" she cried. "And I know I'm not going to like it!"

Sobbing, she ran to the door and out into the hall.

Chapter Eight

The elevator door clanked open at the fourth floor. Erin turned away from the people standing there, certain that her eyes were red and puffy. There was no place to hide.

"By golly, here she is now!" It was Mr. Barnhart, the doughnut maker. "It's the girl I was tellin' you about. Walked right into my place while I was sound asleep. Never would have known she was there if Sailor hadn't spoke up."

He talked as if Erin were an especially sneaky burglar. "I didn't——" she began, but then she saw that Mr. Barnhart was smiling broadly. So were the two elderly women who were with him.

"You're a brave girl," one of the women said. "I wouldn't have known what to do, I'm sure. But then," she sniffed, "I would never put a pan full of oil on the stove and then fall asleep."

Mr. Barnhart seemed unbothered by the criticism. He peered at Erin. "Been cryin', haven't you? Any fool can see that. Bet you're goin' to see our Molly."

"I—I was going for a walk," Erin said, but she stepped out into the hallway. Mr. Barnhart waved his friends into the elevator and seized Erin's arm. "You see Molly," he said firmly. "She'll be good for what ails you."

He walked with Erin to the door of Molly's apartment and waited while she knocked. "Just had a session here myself," he said. "I'm not going to make doughnuts any more. Seems my wife meant salads and frozen dinners—easy stuff like that—when she said I should try to do more cookin' for myself. I s'pose she's right." He grinned. "Always had the last word before she died, and she's still havin' it."

He shuffled back down the hall toward his own apartment, chuckling under his breath. Erin watched him, still not sure this was what she wanted to do. But when he turned back and waved, she knocked again on Molly Panca's door.

"Come in." The voice sounded thin and far away, with only a trace of the lilt Erin recalled. "I'm afraid I can't come to the door."

Erin turned the knob and stepped inside. The little living room was dark, its only light coming from a floor lamp draped in pink cheesecloth. Shades covered the window, and the air was heavy with incense.

"You've come back! Oh, I'm glad."

Molly Panca lay on the flowered couch under a pink sheet. "I've had a busy morning, and it's left me a bit tired," she said. "But I'm delighted to see you again, dear. Sit down in that chair and we'll chat."

Erin did as she was told, but she wished she hadn't let Mr. Barnhart talk her into this. If his friends hadn't stopped the elevator at the fourth floor, she would have gone all the way downstairs and outside. After that— well, she didn't know where she would have gone after that. But at least she wouldn't have had to chat.

"I saw Mr. Barnhart in the hall," she said shyly. "He said it would be all right if I came to see you. But I can't stay long."

"All right! My dear, of course it's all right. Would you like a peach? Or an almond cookie? My children love my almond cookies."

Erin said, "No, thank you." As her eyes became used to the dim light, she saw that Molly's face was almost as white as her crown of curls.

"I do apologize for lying down"—one thin hand stretched toward Erin and then fell back on the sheet— "but our session this morning was quite exhausting. The Brown sisters wanted to get in touch with their mother, as usual, and Mr. Barnhart frightened me half to death with his story about the doughnuts. Are you the young lady who saved us all from going up in smoke?"

Erin nodded. "I guess so. Mr. Barnhart was sleeping, and his parrot called for help. Otherwise I wouldn't have—"

"He told us all about it. He's such a good man, but he does need all the help he can get. He doesn't eat properly, he forgets to change his shirt—oh my!" She smiled, the glowing smile Erin remembered. "That's why I'm so glad I can keep him in touch with his wife."

"You mean—in a seance? You had a seance today?" For a moment Erin forgot her unhappiness.

"That's right. And I do think it was very worthwhile. Mr. Barnhart has promised to try simpler dishes in the future, and Miss Cora Brown is going to see her doctor for a complete checkup right away. Her mother insists on it."

Erin cleared her throat. "You mean—Miss Brown's mother is dead?"

"Of course she's dead, dear," Molly Panca replied. "If she were alive, Miss Brown wouldn't need me, would she?" She rubbed her forehead. "I just wish I didn't tire so easily. And I'm very sorry about your little brother. Was he terribly disappointed?"

"My *brother*?" Erin wondered if she'd heard correctly. "Do you mean Cowper?"

Molly Panca sat up. "Didn't you know he came to see me? Then I'm sure I wasn't supposed to mention it. You won't tell him, will you, Erin dear? I felt so sorry for the poor little tyke."

"He's not my real brother," Erin said. "He's adopted—sort of. Why did he come to see you?"

"He said you showed him my card, and he wants to talk with someone who has passed away. He asked if I'd help him, and I said I'd be glad to if his mother and father said it was all right. I couldn't let a child attend a seance without his parents' permission," she added primly.

Erin tried to remember what Cowper had said when she told her family about meeting Molly Panca. *You'd have to be crazy to think you could talk to dead people, wouldn't you? You'd have to be off the wall.* But he hadn't meant it. He must have started planning right then to visit Molly himself!

"He said he was sure that if he asked, your parents would say no. And then he left." Molly Panca pushed back the sheet and dropped her feet to the rug. She was wearing the poodle skirt again, with a ruffled lavender blouse. Her furry pink slippers had glass eyes and laid-back rabbit ears on the toes.

"I'm sorry I mentioned it," Molly Panca said worriedly. "The child seemed so miserable. I wouldn't want to make him feel worse."

Miserable? Cowper? Erin began to wonder if they were talking about the same person. She could believe her foster brother might worry about doing well in the master class, but he certainly wasn't *miserable*.

"I don't know what he wanted," Erin told Molly,

who was watching her anxiously. "Maybe he wants to talk to his real mother and father. Or maybe"—she had an inspiration—"maybe he wants to talk to Beethoven or Mozart. Music is all he cares about."

Molly Panca looked relieved. "Well, that would be exciting for all of us," she said with a chuckle. Then she changed the subject abruptly. "What are *you* doing for excitement while you're in Milwaukee, Erin?"

Excitement? That was a joke, Erin thought. "We *almost* went to the zoo today," she said crossly. "But then he—Cowper—decided he had to practice the piano, so we couldn't go. He's the reason we're in Milwaukee," she went on when Molly looked puzzled. "He's taking a special piano class at the conservatory, and we all had to come with him. . . ."

"I see." Molly's steady blue gaze suggested she saw a great deal. It was eerie, but she seemed to hear what Erin was saying and what she was not saying as well.

"Of course, I'm glad he's a genius and everything." Erin tried again to be Sara Crewe but failed. "I just don't see why he has to spoil everyone else's fun."

Molly looked as if she were thinking hard. *She's probably going to tell me how mean and jealous I am*, Erin thought. But surprisingly, when her hostess spoke it was to change the subject again.

"As long as you're here, dear, I want you to meet my family. They never get out, and they do love company."

Erin blinked. Was this some kind of joke? She wasn't in the mood for jokes.

"In there," Molly pointed at the bedroom door. "Go right in. Don't be shy. They've been looking out the window all morning, bless their hearts."

Erin went to the door and looked in. Molly Panca's bedroom was as unusual as her living room. There were ruffles everywhere—puffy layers of them around the dressing table and deep flounces on the curtains that framed the windows. The bed was covered with a flow-ered pink spread, and there were clusters of artificial roses and iris attached to the tall bedposts. Pink netting hung from the ceiling to the floor at the head of the bed. Pictures of flowers dotted the walls, and a pair of plaster bluebirds dangled above a chest of drawers.

It was the window that made Erin feel she must be dreaming. A cluster of figures stood on a shelf just below the sill, faces pressed against the glass. There were at least a dozen tiny women, none more than two feet tall, in elegant silk and velvet dresses. The lone man wore a black suit and top hat; he looked out of place in that mass of color. The way the little people stood, intent on the view outside, made them star-tlingly real.

Molly Panca joined Erin at the doorway. "This is Erin Lindsay, my dears. She lives upstairs. Mind your manners and say hello."

There was a whisper of soft "hellos" from the window.

Erin gasped. "But they're dolls!" she protested. "They can't talk!"

"Of course they talk," Molly Panca said crisply. "Now let me see if Margaret Mary is awake." She tiptoed to the bed and peered down at the scattering of pink, blue, and lavender pillows. For the first time Erin saw a doll figure lying among them.

"We have company, Margaret Mary. Erin Lindsay has come to meet you." Molly lifted the doll tenderly and propped her among the pillows, smoothing the full white skirt and adjusting the white sunbonnet. The strap of a tiny white leather suitcase was wrapped around her wrist.

"Margaret Mary usually prefers the living room window," Molly said. "Don't you, dear? But I do think she should join the others at the window today. There's a bulldozer clearing the lot next door, and it's a marvelous sight."

"Well, I'm not going to push and shove to get a place," Margaret Mary snapped. "If the earl wants me there, he can tell the others to make room for me. Otherwise, I'd rather catch up on my sleep."

If Molly saw Erin's stunned expression, she pretended not to notice. "That's the earl of Kirby she's talking about," she whispered and pointed at the man doll. "I'm afraid Margaret Mary is just a teeny bit jealous."

"I am *not* jealous," Margaret Mary retorted. "I just want someone to think about *me* for a change. Please go away and leave me alone."

Molly sighed and retreated to the living room, drawing Erin behind her. "I'm sorry the children aren't more sociable," she said. "Ordinarily, they'd be thrilled to have a visitor, but that bulldozer . . . And I've never known Margaret Mary to be so rude. She spoils her own good times, poor child."

Erin slumped into the armchair. "How do you do that?" she asked. "How do you make them talk?"

Molly seemed puzzled by the question. "I don't *make* them talk," she protested. "But if they want to talk, I don't stop them. And I am truly sorry about Margaret Mary. One shouldn't have favorites, but I can't help it. Usually she's very good company, but today she's missing the fun, and it has put her in a bad temper. Especially since it's her own fault she's left out. She wants all of the earl's attention, or she's unhappy. Jealousy is a dreadful thing, don't you agree?"

Erin looked at Molly Panca suspiciously. If there was a hidden message in this conversation, the sweet, pale face gave no sign of it.

"Well, I'm sorry for Margaret Mary," Erin said defiantly. "It isn't her fault she feels bad. She knows no one's worried about *her* feelings. She has a right to be grumpy."

Molly Panca smiled her glowing, innocent smile. "It doesn't matter whose fault it is," she said gently. "Margaret Mary is the one who's missing the fun."

I'm as weird as she is, Erin thought. *We're both talking as if Margaret Mary's a real person.*

"I just wish she'd let herself have a good time instead of sulking," Molly continued. "It's too late for some of us, but Margaret Mary is young and strong. . . ."

Erin went back to the bedroom door for one more look at Molly's family. They were still crowded around the window—of course. They were dolls, and they stayed where they were put. Margaret Mary lay among the pink, blue, and lavender pillows. She was a doll, too.

"I do wish you'd go away, Erin Lindsay," the doll on the bed said clearly. "If I want to feel sorry for myself, that's my business." And though her lips didn't move, the pretty doll face wore a pouting expression.

Chapter Nine

"No big mystery there." Mr. Lindsay helped himself to another slice of meat loaf. "The woman's a ventriloquist—a pretty good one, I'd say, if she could give Erin the impression that a whole crowd of dolls was saying hello."

"She's not a ventriloquist!" Erin saw her mother's warning look and softened her voice. "You don't know Molly. If you did, you wouldn't say that. She wouldn't play a trick on me."

"I'm sure she doesn't think of it as a trick," Mrs. Lindsay said. "Your friend is probably very lonely. This building is full of lonely old people. And I'm sure the dolls are just like real people to Miss Panca. They *are* her family. If she's a ventriloquist, it's not surprising that she'd use her talent to make them more real. You can understand that, can't you?"

Erin didn't want to listen, even though she knew her

parents might be right. Molly Panca was an unusual person. She didn't dress like anyone else, and her apartment was different. She talked to dead people. Maybe she was a ventriloquist, too.

"It's a talent that would come in handy in a seance," Mr. Lindsay said thoughtfully. "Think about it. Being able to throw your voice would be very good for business."

"She doesn't talk to spirits for money!" Erin exclaimed, angry all over again. "She does it to help her friends."

"Still . . ." Mr. Lindsay patted his mouth with a paper napkin and leaned back in his chair. "Just don't take it all too seriously, my queen," he said. "I don't mean Molly's a bad person. But it does sound to me as if she has a few tricks up her sleeve and doesn't mind using them."

"The stone lion," Cowper said suddenly. He'd been pushing his food around on his plate, hardly eating anything.

"What about the lion?" Erin demanded.

"Uncle Jack told me about the stone lion who talked. Molly Panca's apartment is at the front of this building, right?"

As if you didn't know. Erin narrowed her eyes at him. "So?"

"So her windows overlook the entrance. Maybe she

saw you sitting down there next to the lion, looking bored, and she decided to surprise you."

"Now *you're* saying she played a trick on me," Erin protested. "It's not true! She isn't like that. She's a nice person. You—" She'd been about to say, "You've met her," but caught herself in time. She'd promised Molly not to let Cowbird know that Molly had mentioned his visit.

Cowper shrugged as if it didn't matter whether Erin believed him or not. "So she's a nice person," he said. "She's a nice person who likes to help people. Whatever way she can."

Later, after Cowper had gone down the hall to his bedroom and Erin was taking her turn with the dinner dishes, she heard her parents talking in the living room.

"Well, at least he spoke up at dinner tonight," Mrs. Lindsay said in a low voice. "He's been terribly quiet ever since he came home from his practice session this afternoon. Even quieter than usual."

The newspaper rattled. "Nerves," Erin's father muttered. "He's worked himself up into a state about that audition. As if Salzman would let him try it if he wasn't good enough!"

"Sometimes I wonder what's going on inside that boy's head," Mrs. Lindsay said. "I love him to pieces, but I feel as if I hardly know him. Do you know what I mean?"

"Mmm." More rattling of newspaper.

Erin waited, but the conversation was over. There was nothing about loving their daughter to pieces. No talk about what was going on in *her* head. Why should they worry about their ordinary child when they had a genius to think about?

Erin scrunched the dishcloth into a little ball, her knuckles gleaming white through the start of a summer tan. When Rufus unexpectedly brushed against her ankles, she almost screamed.

"I wish Cowbird was dead!" The ugly words shot out like bullets, horrifying Erin, even though there was no one to hear but Rufus. The big cat darted away.

"I didn't mean that," she whispered quickly. "I didn't mean it at all. I just wish he wasn't part of this family. I wish he was *gone*."

Rufus returned and stretched out at her feet, waiting to have his stomach rubbed, but Erin just looked at him. Saying those dreadful words had put a wall between her and the rest of the world. She was sure the ugliness inside her must show. No one would love her, if they knew what she was really like.

Not even Rufus.

The next morning was a long one. Cowper stayed home from class to get ready for his two o'clock audition. Instead of resting, he wandered around the apartment like a zombie before finally disappearing into his room. Erin tried to start on her video script, but her great ideas had vanished, and new ones refused to come. She jumped when her father came into the living room.

"I think," he said somberly, "this would be a good time to tell your brother you're ready to be friends."

She panicked. Could her parents have heard the awful thing she'd said in the kitchen last night?

"I'm sure he feels bad about making you miss the zoo trip yesterday," her father went on. "It's worrying him, and besides that he seems pretty concerned about the audition this afternoon. You'd make him feel a lot better if you'd tell him you're not still mad."

Relief flooded over Erin. He hadn't heard. "I'll do it now," she said and tossed her notebook aside. Maybe she could help herself to feel better at the same time.

When Erin knocked on Cowper's bedroom door, there was a scrambling sound and then a soft "Okay." He was at the window, his face so closed and private-looking that she almost changed her mind about making up.

"What's the matter?" he asked warily.

"Nothing. I just wanted to say"—she forced herself to go on—"it's okay about the zoo. We'll go some other time. And I hope—I hope you do all right at your audition."

"Thanks." The closed expression slipped away, and

now he just looked unhappy. Miserable. "But I won't," he said.

"Won't what?"

"I won't do all right. I know it." Cowper's voice cracked. "Listen," he said tensely, "would you ask that—Molly if she'll let me come to a seance? I know Uncle Jack says it's just ventriloquism and tricks, but maybe he's wrong. I went to see her myself, but she said I couldn't be at a seance unless Uncle Jack and Aunt Grace said it was okay. And I know they won't."

"You said Molly was playing tricks, too," Erin said accusingly. "Who do you want to talk to at the seance, anyway?"

"My mom and dad. I have to ask them something. I have to!"

"Ask them what?"

The Look returned, and Cowper stared out the window. "Just tell me if you'll ask Molly," he said stubbornly. "I need to know."

"Okay." Erin doubted it would do any good, but she couldn't say no. This was a Cowper she'd never seen before. "We can go downstairs and see her right now if you want to."

"Right!" Cowper was across the room and halfway down the hall before Erin could move—unflappable Cowbird who usually did everything at his own slow, steady pace!

Mr. Lindsay smiled approvingly when Erin told him

she and Cowper were going to see Molly Panca together. "Good girl!" he exclaimed. "Maybe a change of scene will help."

Five minutes later they were knocking at Molly's door. "Come in, come in," her sweet voice trilled, and her face lit up like a child's when she saw them. "How wonderful! We were just hoping someone would drop by, weren't we, darlings?"

Margaret Mary and the earl of Kirby were sitting side by side at one end of the couch, facing Molly at the other. Molly looked like a princess, Erin thought, a beautiful old princess. She wore a long silky robe with bluebirds all over it.

"It's nice to have a little male company," the earl of Kirby said. His voice was deep and pleasant. "Not that these ladies aren't charming, of course."

Erin glanced at Cowper. His mouth hung open, and his eyes were unbelieving. Obviously, he hadn't met any of Molly's family on his first visit.

"I've just told one of my favorite stories," Margaret Mary announced. "Sit down and I'll tell it again."

Erin sank to the floor, cross-legged, and Cowper backed into the nearest chair without taking his eyes from the dolls.

"I don't think we'll have the story again right now," Molly said gently. "I believe our friends have come for a reason. Am I right?"

Cowper, still staring at the dolls, seemed unable to

speak, so Erin answered for him. "What we wanted to know was whether you'd let Cowper come to a seance. See, his real mother and father died two years ago, and he needs to talk to them about something important."

Cowper tore his gaze away from Margaret Mary and the earl. "Just one question," he pleaded. "That's all."

Molly Panca sat very still. "What is the question, dear?"

He took a deep breath. "I want to know—I want to know if my mom and dad would care if I quit playing the piano. For a while."

Erin scrambled to her knees to face him. "Quit!" she exclaimed. "I thought you loved playing the piano."

"I do," Cowper said softly. "But not all the time. I mean, if it's okay with *them*, I'd like to sort of slow down."

Erin could hardly believe what she was hearing. Even though she was sick-*sick*-SICK of having a genius in the family, it was scary to discover Cowper was sick of it, too.

"Have you told Erin's mother and father how you feel?" Molly asked. "I think they'd want to know."

"Of course he's told them," the earl of Kirby interrupted. "No sense in keeping a thing like that to yourself."

Cowper was speechless again. He shook his head confusedly, looking first at the earl, then at Molly.

"My mother and father want him to be famous," Erin explained.

"Nevertheless, old chap," the earl said firmly, "you have to speak up. It's necessary."

"I always do," Margaret Mary said. "Ask anybody."

"About the seance," Erin said. "Do you think you could . . ."

Molly looked regretful. "I'm sorry, I just can't allow it unless your parents say it's all right, Erin. I'd like to help, but they might be very angry if I said yes. You understand, don't you?"

Cowper slid out of his chair, his expression blank again. "Sure," he said. "Thanks anyway." He turned to Erin. "I guess we'd better go home now so I can get ready for this afternoon."

"You have a special afternoon coming up?" Margaret Mary said brightly. "Lucky old you."

Cowper didn't smile. "Yeah, lucky," he said.

Trailing after him, Erin wished Molly would say something cheering before they left, but it was the earl of Kirby who had the last word as they went out the door. "Don't forget, old chap—speak up. That's what makes a real man."

"Or a real woman," Margaret Mary called after the door had closed behind them. "Ask anybody."

Chapter Ten

"So what are you going to do?" Erin whispered, as they let themselves into the apartment. She felt strange, now that she knew Cowper's incredible secret. All this time she'd been resenting him because his piano playing was the most important thing in their lives. Now, it turned out, he didn't like it any better than she did.

Cowper pretended not to hear her question, and suddenly Erin wanted to shake him. He wouldn't do anything to help himself. It was easier to go along with what other people wanted.

The morning mail was spread on the hall table. Erin skimmed through it and found a letter from Heather— at last. She snatched it up and hurried back to her bedroom. The sight of Heather's handwriting made her more homesick than ever. Quickly, she slit the envelope and skimmed over the contents, trying to swallow all the news in one big bite.

Most of the letter was devoted to the trip to the

haunted schoolhouse. "We waited till dark, but the ghost didn't show up. And then when we got home, my mom changed her mind about letting us go to the horror movie. The sleepover was fun though, even if nobody's ghost stories are as spooky as yours. . . ."

So it hadn't been the scariest night of their lives after all. *But at least Heather and Emily and Meg were together,* Erin thought wistfully. She read on. "We're going to Emily's next Friday. Her dad likes to rent spooky movies, so I know we can watch them there. And we're going to sleep in that big old attic over the garage. It'll be the scariest night ever. Wish you could be there. . . ."

Erin sighed. Well, at least she had her video to think about. As soon as it was finished she'd send it to Heather, maybe in time for next week's sleepover. If it was as terrific as she wanted it to be, she'd make another, and then another—a whole series starring Erin Lindsay, Ghost Detective.

Lunch was quiet, with Cowper refusing even to come to the table.

"Too nervous," Mr. Lindsay reported after a quick visit to the back bedroom. "I wish your mother was home. I guess Molly Hanky-Panky didn't do much for his state of mind, huh?"

Erin kept her eyes on her cheese-and-pickle sandwich. "Guess not."

"Well, he'll be all right after this afternoon is over."

Erin said nothing. If she told her father what Cowper had said to Molly about quitting, he'd dismiss it as "nerves." If she told her mother, she'd say Erin was jealous and was trying to find a way to get them back to Clinton. It was up to Cowper to do his own telling.

After lunch Erin settled down in her room and began working on the video script in earnest.

Important rule: Don't have more than three people in a scene. Someone has to handle the camcorder.

In the first scene, Mr. and Mrs.—she thought a moment, then wrote "Dooley"; that was Heather's last name—Mr. and Mrs. Dooley would visit Detective Lindsay's office to tell her about the weird events that had begun when they moved into their apartment. And after that there would be a long scene in which the brave detective spends a night in the apartment by herself. The scariest night of her life!

Erin chuckled as she jotted down all the bloodcurdling experiences Detective Lindsay was going to have. There would be loud knocking in the walls and papers fluttering mysteriously on a desk. (Someone could stand out of range of the camera and point the hair dryer at the papers to make them move.) With colorless nylon thread a vase could be made to slide off a table, and a picture could shift on the wall. A closed door might open all by itself (with the help of her father or Cowper hidden behind it).

And then the most horrifying moment of all—the

discovery of a corpse lying on the floor! That would be
Cowper. She would turn away—to pick up her camera
and photograph the evidence, maybe?—and when she
would look back, the corpse would be gone.

Who is the ghost-corpse? Why is he haunting the
Dooleys' apartment? It would be up to clever Detective
Lindsay to find the answers. Erin nibbled the end of her
pencil and considered different possibilities. Maybe
. . . maybe . . . Her pencil flew over the page with a
perfect solution to the mystery. It would mean Cowper
must play two parts instead of one, but he would have
to do it. She'd gone with him to visit Molly Panca, so
he owed her a favor, didn't he?

She worked for another hour before she stopped. The
script was complete. *Wait till Heather and Meg and
Emily see this!* she thought. It might be corny but it
would be fun. If she couldn't be there with them to tell
ghost stories, the video would be the next best thing.

The apartment was silent when she opened her bedroom door. Rufus followed her down the hall to the
living room, where they found Mrs. Lindsay reading a
textbook. She put the book aside and rubbed her eyes
wearily when Erin came in.

"Your door was closed when I got home from class,
so I didn't bother you. Were you taking a nap?"

"Writing." Erin tried to sound offhand. "My
script."

"Wonderful!" Her mother sounded genuinely

pleased. "You look as if you've had a satisfying afternoon. Now if we can just say the same about your
brother . . . They should be home from the audition
any time now."

She'd hardly said the words when a key turned in the
lock and the hall door opened. Rufus leaped to the back
of the couch, and they all stared expectantly as Cowper
and Mr. Lindsay came into the living room.

Erin's father was smiling, but it wasn't a relaxed,
let's-celebrate grin. Cowper looked terrible. He shot
Erin a glance of pure pain and then stared at the floor
as if he'd never seen a flowered carpet before.

"Goodness!" Mrs. Lindsay's voice sounded strained.
"Is everything all right?"

"Sure is," Erin's father replied, too heartily. "Cowper thinks he didn't do his best work, but I'm sure he's
worrying for nothing. I'm sure—"

"I stopped," Cowper interrupted. "Right in the middle of the second movement."

"You mean you forgot?" Erin was astonished. Cowper never worried about forgetting; it had always
seemed to her that the music must be inside him just
waiting to be played.

Cowper's face flushed a dark red.

"But he started right up again," Mr. Lindsay said
quickly. "That kind of thing could happen to
anybody—doesn't mean a thing."

Mrs. Lindsay took a deep breath. "What did the person from the university say?"

"That's Mr. Corini. He conducts the symphony orchestra. He's going to give us a call tomorrow and tell us the good news."

Cowper looked as if he might throw up. "I'm going to lie down for a while," he said. "I'm sort of tired."

Mrs. Lindsay jumped up and went with him down the hall.

"It wasn't as bad as he thinks," Erin's father said. He threw himself into a chair and stretched his long legs. "He wants to be perfect—that's the problem. Nothing matters except playing the piano."

Erin marveled that her father, who knew so much, could be all wrong about Cowper. She wondered what it would take to make him see the truth.

"Look," he said now, "I was just thinking—how's that play of yours coming along?"

"My video," Erin said. "It's all finished. The script, I mean."

"Great!" He sat up. "How about putting your actors to work tomorrow? Your mother doesn't have classes in the morning, and maybe I can take a day off. We'll suggest that Cowper skip one more class, too. What do you say?"

"Tomorrow!" Erin was pleased with his enthusiasm, but she'd counted on more time to plan the weird things the ghost would do to frighten Detective Lindsay and get her attention. "Can't we wait a couple more days?"

"The thing is," Mr. Lindsay said, "Corini will probably call in the morning about the audition. If he doesn't think Cowper's ready to do a concert, the poor kid's going to feel terrible. I thought if we all got busy on something together, we could take his mind off his troubles."

So that was it. Her father wasn't really interested in the video; he just wanted to keep Cowper busy. Erin started to say she couldn't possibly be ready tomorrow, but then she remembered how Cowper had looked when he came home from the audition. She didn't want to feel sorry for him, but she couldn't help it.

"Okay," she said reluctantly. "I guess it'll be all right."

Her father leaned back and smiled at her. "Terrific!" he said. "We can always depend on you, my queen."

Hearing that ought to help, Erin thought. Sara Crewe would be happy if someone said that to her. *But I don't want to be dependable, I want to be special.*

Like Cowbird.

Chapter Eleven

The sky was just beginning to turn gray when Erin switched off her alarm, slipped into jeans and a top, and tiptoed down the hall. She planned to use her bedroom for Detective Lindsay's office, but most of the video would take place in the living room. She'd left some spools of thread on the coffee table the night before, and now she set right to work. For what seemed like hours last night, she'd planned the "tricks" that the ghost could play.

By the time Erin's parents and Cowper wandered down the hall, she was ready. Standing at the door, she could make a vase slide mysteriously across a table, simply by tugging on a length of invisible nylon thread. Another piece of thread, double strength, made a footstool tip over. The heavy painting over the couch slid sideways with a couple of tugs; a little metal plate fell off its shelf with a startling *smack*.

"What're you doing?" Cowper asked dully.

"Watch," Erin said. She crouched and pulled a thread. The pottery vase full of fake flowers began to move slowly toward the edge of the end table.

Cowper's eyes widened. "How'd you do that?" he demanded.

Erin showed him the thread wrapped around her finger. "You and Mom and Dad are going to have to do all the tricks," she said. "I'll be acting." She'd practiced looking scared in front of the mirror before she went to bed last night.

Cowper picked up another thread and gave it a tentative pull. The painting over the couch slipped sideways. "What else?" he asked. "This is fun."

"I'll show you later," Erin told him, relieved that he seemed willing to help. "You're going to have a little extra acting to do," she said cautiously. "That'll be fun, too."

Cowper dropped the thread. "You said I could be a dead body," he said. "That's all I'm going to do. I don't know how to be an actor."

Erin frowned. She didn't want to argue with him before they even started the video, but she felt her temper rising. Fortunately, Mrs. Lindsay chose that minute to call them to breakfast.

"Okay," Erin's father said after his first sip of coffee. "Tell us what's going to happen this morning, Madame Director."

Erin hadn't forgiven him for being interested in the video only as a means of entertaining Cowper. Still, when she began explaining the plot, she couldn't hide her excitement. "You're Mr. and Mrs. Dooley," she told her parents. "They're nice, but they're kind of chicken—I mean timid."

"Thanks a lot," her father said dryly. "I won't have to act much. I'll just be my plain old chicken self."

"Spooky things start happening in their apartment, so they go to see a famous ghost-detective," Erin hurried on. "That's me. And the detective decides to spend some time in the apartment all alone to see what she can find out. The Dooleys go away so she can have the apartment to herself."

"Good!" Mrs. Lindsay-Dooley exclaimed. "I'm much too timid to be of any help."

Erin described the ghostly tricks she had planned. "The very last thing that happens," she explained, "is that the detective starts searching the apartment, and she discovers a body lying on the floor."

"That's you, Cowper," Mr. Lindsay announced. "The part you wanted."

Cowper didn't smile. He was watching Erin uneasily.

"But then the body disappears," Erin went on. "Because it isn't real. And when Detective Lindsay describes the ghost-corpse to the Dooleys, they say it sounds like the man whose apartment they're renting. He's a very rich, famous author who is away on a trip doing research for his next book."

"Mysteriouser and mysteriouser!" Mr. Lindsay exclaimed. "Now what does Detective Lindsay do?"

"Well, at first she doesn't know what to think." Erin wrinkled her forehead, pretending to concentrate. "But then she notices a book lying on the coffee table, and it's the story the famous author has written about his own life. She opens it up, and there on the very first page"—she paused and looked around triumphantly—"he says he had an identical twin brother. The brother was adopted the day they were born, and the author has never seen him again."

"So what?" Cowper demanded. "What's the twin brother got to do with it?"

"I know!" Mrs. Lindsay's eyes sparkled. "The brother has come back and killed the author. He's taken the author's place and has taken all his money as well. And the author can't rest in peace because his murderer hasn't been caught. That's why his ghost—I mean his ghost-corpse—is haunting the apartment. Erin, what a marvelous idea!"

"My daughter the writer!" Erin's father slapped the table so hard they all jumped. "You're going to be a rich, famous author yourself, my queen!"

Erin looked at Cowper. He looked—she could hardly

believe it—he looked impressed. "That's pretty good,"
he said slowly. "I don't know how you made up a thing
like that."

Then the uneasy expression came back. "What happens next?"

Erin hesitated. They all liked the plot so far, even
Cowper. He *had* to agree to the rest of it. "While
they're talking there's a knock at the door, and it's
the brother—the murderer-brother. He's home from
his trip, and he's come to collect the rent. And he
looks exactly like the ghost-corpse. So Detective
Lindsay accuses him of murder. And when she shows
him the book, he tries to run away, but she—she
tackles him—"

"Oh my," Mrs. Lindsay breathed. "Does she have
to?"

"They can fake it," Erin's father said. "Cowper can
pretend to fall. Can't you, Cowper?"

Before he could answer, the telephone rang. Mr.
Lindsay pushed back his chair. "I'll get it," he said
lightly. "Probably some salesman."

"It's probably Mr. Corini," Cowper said. He leaned
back in his chair, his face as white as Margaret Mary's
bonnet, his arms folded across his chest.

"Now, let's not get all upset about this," Mrs. Lindsay said. "After all . . ." Her voice trailed off, and they
waited in silence.

It seemed a very long time before Mr. Lindsay returned. "You were right, Cowper," he said. "That was Mr. Corini himself."

"What'd he say?" Cowper barely breathed the words.

"He said you're a remarkable young player, and he enjoyed hearing you. He was impressed. And he hopes to have you perform with the symphony—someday."

"When?" Erin's mother asked.

Mr. Lindsay cleared his throat. "Oh, a few years from now," he said. "When Cowper's a little older. More experienced." He reached across the table and ruffled Cowper's hair. "That means we can forget about the audition and concentrate on Erin's video," he said heartily. "What do you say?"

Not a chance, Erin thought. Any second now, Cowper was going to head down the hall to his bedroom, and that would be the last they'd see of him for the day.

"I don't think Cowper feels like acting at the moment," Mrs. Lindsay said. "Erin understands, don't you, dear?"

Cowper had been sitting very still, staring at nothing at all. Now he blinked and shook his head. "I'm okay," he said in a small voice. "I can do it."

Erin was astonished, and judging by her parents' expressions, they were surprised, too.

Mr. Lindsay recovered first. "Well, great!" he exclaimed. "Let's get to work then. Madame Director?"

He bowed in Erin's direction, and they all filed after him out of the kitchen.

It was a morning Erin would remember. At first she felt uncomfortable telling her mother and father what to do and what to say when they came to Detective Lindsay's office. Cowper had to be shown exactly how to hold the camcorder and warned not to move it around too much or too fast. Being the director meant being the boss.

But the awkwardness slipped away when they started the scene. Mr. Lindsay was convincing and funny as the timid Mr. Dooley. He stammered nervously as he told the detective about their haunted apartment. Mrs. Lindsay–Dooley nodded in agreement and whispered, "That's right" and "Gracious me, it was *horrible!*" whenever he paused.

When the first scene was complete, they trooped from Erin's bedroom to the living room. Now Erin turned the camcorder over to her mother and demonstrated all of her ghost-tricks for her father and Cowper.

Mr. Lindsay was as impressed as Cowper had been earlier. "You've done a terrific job," he said and pulled the nearest thread. A pillow moved on the couch as if an invisible hand had touched it.

Cowper didn't say much, but he listened carefully to Erin's explanations and even volunteered to hide behind the armchair and make it "rock."

By the time everyone had their assignments clearly in mind, it was nearly noon. "Let's take a break," Mrs. Lindsay suggested. "I need some lunch if I'm going to do a good job as the cameraperson."

"Excellent idea," Mr. Lindsay agreed. "I always act better after I've had a bologna sandwich. What do you say, Cowper?"

"It's okay with me." He was strangely calm, Erin thought, almost as if he'd forgotten the bad news from Mr. Corini. But she knew he hadn't. He was thinking about it and thinking about it. Any minute now he might say he was tired and didn't want to work on the video anymore.

"About the last scene," Erin said, when they were settled at the kitchen table eating their sandwiches. "We could—"

She stopped when her mother put up a warning hand. "No shoptalk at the table," she said firmly. "Time to relax." She smiled when she said it, but Erin could tell her parents were wondering what Cowper was thinking, too.

As soon as lunch was over, they went back to the living room. Erin closed the draperies and turned on the lamps, then lay down on the couch, pretending to doze. After a moment or two the pillow twitched under her head, and she opened her eyes in pretended astonishment.

"What's going on?" She sat up, just as some papers on the coffee table floated to the floor. Then a thunderous knocking shook the walls, and a low moan floated through the room.

Detective Lindsay was cool and brave. "I have to find out the reason for all this," she muttered. "I'd better search the whole apartment." She tiptoed across the living room, aware that her mother was right behind her with the camcorder.

When she stepped out into the hall, the ghost-corpse was lying where they'd planned, but with a difference. Cowper had covered himself with a long white bath-towel, in order to look "ghostly." His eyes were wide open, and his lips were parted in a truly frightening grin.

Detective Lindsay dropped her flashlight in surprise. When she picked it up, the corpse had vanished.

Mrs. Lindsay switched off the camcorder, and Cowper reappeared in the kitchen doorway. "How was I?" he demanded. "Did I look dead?"

Mrs. Lindsay made a face. "Very."

"Well, that's good." Cowper turned to Erin. "You'd better tell me the rest of my lines. And we'll have to practice the fight so it looks real."

Erin stared at him. She was aware of her father listening in the front hall and her mother close by, not moving. She knew they were thinking the same thing she was. *Cowper isn't just pretending—he's having fun. And he wants to play the part of the murderer!*

"We have one more scene to do first," Erin explained carefully. "Mr. and Mrs. Dooley come home, and Detective Lindsay finds the book about the famous author's life, and she figures out who the killer is. That won't take long. And then we'll practice the fight, okay?"

"Okay." Cowper took the camcorder from Mrs. Lindsay and hoisted it to his shoulder. "I like doing this, too." He ambled into the living room, pointing the camera in one direction and then another.

Erin followed, and her mother and father brought up the rear. "Detective Lindsay, you're a miracle worker," her father whispered. "What's going on here?"

"I don't know," Erin whispered back, giggling. She didn't feel like a miracle worker, but it was nice to be called one.

Then she surprised herself with a totally unexpected thought. It was nice to have a brother.

Chapter Twelve

Cowper made his announcement that night at the Burger Boy across from the YMCA. Mr. Lindsay had decided they must go out for supper to celebrate the finishing of "the world's most terrifying video."

"We've earned it," he said, as they settled into a booth in the brightly lit restaurant. "Mr. and Mrs. Dooley are exhausted, and the two of you must be black and blue." He looked from Erin to Cowper. "It was a terrific fight, though. It looked very convincing when we played it back."

"As long as you didn't hurt your hands, Cowper," Mrs. Lindsay said. "All those practice falls . . ." She shook her head. "What's the matter, dear?"

Cowper leaned back against the purple cushions. "The thing is," he said slowly, "it doesn't matter about my hands. Because I want to stop playing the piano."

Erin held her breath. He was actually saying it.

"You want—what?" Mrs. Lindsay looked dazed. "I don't understand."

"I want to stop playing the piano," Cowper repeated. He began tearing his paper napkin into tiny pieces. "For a while, anyway."

"But you can't! What are you talking about, Cowper? You have so much talent. . . ." Erin's mother leaned across the table and took the shredded napkin from his fingers. "You're just discouraged, dear. And you're tired. You'll feel different tomorrow."

"No, I won't. I feel fine. I just want to do something else for a while."

"What?" Mr. Lindsay exploded. "What in the world do you want to do?"

Cowper shrugged. "I don't know," he said. "Just something else." He looked sideways at Erin. "We could make another video maybe. Or I could learn how to skateboard. Stuff like that."

"But you love music! You've always loved it."

Cowper kicked the leg of the table, a steady tap-tap-tap. "I still do," he said. "But I don't want to play the piano all the time. I'm tired of *that*."

A waitress approached the table, but Mr. Lindsay waved her away. He reached across the table to squeeze Cowper's shoulder. "You don't have to do anything you don't want to do," he said. "But before you make up your mind, let me tell you how your Aunt Grace and I feel. We know you're working very hard this summer, but it's only for a couple of months. We're trying to help you the way your mom and dad would have if they were here. You don't want to let them down, I know, and neither do we. We want you to get better and better, just the way they hoped you would. If you stick with it, you *will* be a famous concert pianist some day."

It was a long speech. *And no jokes*, Erin thought. She'd never seen her father so intent. As Cowper listened, his defiant look faded. It seemed to Erin that he was shrinking into the purple cushions.

"Uncle Jack is right," Mrs. Lindsay joined in. "Music has been the most important thing in the world to you, dear. We know you were disappointed today, but you've been very brave about it. And there'll be other auditions, lots of them. We're counting on you. Uncle Jack is and I am, and so are your own mother and father. Erin's counting on you, too."

"Not me," Erin said quickly. "If he really doesn't want to play anymore—" Her mother's reproachful look stopped her.

Cowper picked up a menu. "It's okay," he said softly. "I was just kidding, anyway. I'll have a cheeseburger and a strawberry shake, okay?"

"Okay!" Mr. Lindsay said. "Good idea. I'll have the same. What about the ladies?"

While they gave their orders to the waitress, Erin

watched her parents curiously. Couldn't they see that Cowper hadn't been kidding? Couldn't *he* see that he'd have to try harder than that to convince her parents he was serious?

A half hour later Erin and Cowper stood side by side in the parking lot waiting for their parents, who had stopped to talk to someone from the university.

"Why are you such a chicken?" Erin demanded. "First you tell them the truth, and then you pretend you didn't mean it. That's dumb!"

Cowper gave her The Look. "It won't work," he said sullenly. "I tried to do what the earl—that *doll*—said to do, but it didn't help. They don't want to know how I feel."

"They do," Erin argued. "You didn't try hard enough. They think you're just feeling bad about the audition."

Cowper turned to her. "I'll tell you something," he said earnestly. "The audition was a kind of test, see? When Mr. Corini said I wasn't good enough to play in a concert—well, that meant it was okay to tell Uncle Jack and Aunt Grace I wanted to quit for a while. All day long I had fun because I thought it was going to be okay. I thought they'd understand. But they didn't. You heard them. If I quit, they'll hate me."

Erin was outraged. "They will not! They're not like that."

Cowper started across the parking lot toward the car. "You don't know," he said. "*You* can do anything you want to do." He plodded away from her and climbed into the back seat of the car.

That's a laugh! Erin thought fiercely. *I can't do what I want to do. Today was great, but from now on it's going to be day after day of* Nothing.

She actually felt worse because Cowper had tried to make her parents understand and had failed. *He'll never say it again*, she thought dismally. *My whole life's going to be ruined because he won't tell the truth. It's not fair*!

During the week that followed, the family acted as if the conversation at the Burger Boy had never happened. Cowper went to the conservatory every day, and if he was even quieter than usual, no one but Erin seemed to notice. Her parents continued to take turns driving him to school and going to their own classes at the university. Erin mailed her video to Heather; after that she felt lost. In the mornings she read, watched television, and wrote long letters to her friends in Clinton. Afternoons she wandered downstairs to visit Molly Panca.

"How's your brother?" the earl of Kirby wanted to know. "I'm a bit worried about him."

Erin shrugged. "He's all right."

"Well, I hope he learns to speak up," the earl said. "Has to do that, you know."

"He tried but it didn't work," Erin said reluctantly. She didn't want to talk about Cowper; she didn't want to think about him.

"You must bring him back for another visit sometime," Molly said sweetly. "The earl enjoyed talking to him."

"Where's Margaret Mary?" Erin asked abruptly. She felt as if she and Margaret Mary understood each other. Of course, Margaret Mary was just a doll, but she was so outspoken, so completely different from Molly Panca, that it was almost impossible to believe that she wasn't wholly and truly a person herself.

From then on Margaret Mary was sitting in the living room with Molly each day when Erin came to call. "I was hoping you'd come," she'd say. Or, "I thought you'd never get here! I've been bored out of my mind!"

Erin always nodded sympathetically. Her head ached from hours of watching the soaps and game shows.

"I want to go somewhere exciting," Margaret Mary would exclaim. "I want to have adventures!"

"I'm sure you will, dear," Molly replied soothingly. "Someday it will be your turn. But right now you have this whole beautiful afternoon to enjoy. Don't waste it complaining. You can play games with the others, or you can look out the window—or you can tell us a story. That would be lovely."

"I don't feel like playing games. I'm too unhappy to tell stories."

"You're so young and strong," Molly said wistfully. "It's hard for me to understand how you can be unhappy."

One afternoon Margaret Mary was even fuller of complaints than usual. "The earl doesn't pay any attention to me," she whined. "He doesn't care what I do."

And my mom and dad would rather think about Cowbird than about me. The words popped into Erin's head, unbidden. "I'd better go home," she said uncomfortably. "I have some things to do."

"What things?" Margaret Mary demanded. "You're going to have fun, I suppose."

"I don't—" Erin hesitated. She'd been about to say, "I don't have any fun," but there was no way to say the words without sounding exactly like Margaret Mary. Whiny. Sulky. A pain in the neck.

"You're trying to teach me a lesson," she accused Molly. "Just because you know I'd rather be in Clinton than stuck here in Milwaukee . . ."

Molly Panca shook her head. "I'm too tired to teach anybody a lesson," she said with a weary little laugh. "Come back tomorrow, and maybe we'll all feel better—you and me and Margaret Mary, too."

Erin wanted to say *she* wouldn't feel any better, but that too sounded like Margaret Mary. Besides, she knew that when tomorrow came, she'd be back knocking on Molly's door.

"I picked up a schedule of activities at the YWCA,"

Mrs. Lindsay said that night. "There's a beginning gymnastics class on Wednesdays and Fridays. That sounds interesting, doesn't it? And how about this—a drama group on Wednesday mornings. You liked being in plays at school, Erin. Maybe they'd be interested in hearing about your video."

"I liked the Drama Club because I knew everybody," Erin said. "And we had good plays."

"Well, it wouldn't hurt to check it out," her father commented. "I'll take you over there if you want me to."

Erin didn't want him to. "Tomorrow morning?" she asked innocently. She knew he had classes tomorrow. "Mom said the drama group meets Wednesday mornings."

Mr. Lindsay looked trapped. "Well maybe not tomorrow morning," he said. "But we can work something out."

Erin returned to her mystery book.

"Between you and your brother!" Mrs. Lindsay said crossly. "Neither one of you knows when you're well off."

Erin looked up. Her parents hardly ever criticized Cowbird. But, of course, she realized her mother wasn't actually criticizing him. She was beginning to notice how quiet he was, and she was worried about him.

"If he doesn't snap out of this mood pretty soon,

we'll have to talk to Mr. Salzman," she continued. "It isn't natural for a child to spend all his spare time in his room alone."

"I think he's just tired," Erin's father said. "He's putting in pretty long days, you know." He was worried, too.

For a moment—only a moment—Erin allowed herself to hope. Maybe Cowbird hadn't given up after all. Maybe he was back there in his bedroom trying to figure how to get out of the master class. Maybe—But then she remembered the way he'd looked at her in the parking lot of the Burger Boy. He *had* given up. He was going to do what he thought his real parents and his foster parents expected him to do. He wasn't a fighter, and he never would be.

The next afternoon Erin slipped away to Molly Panca's apartment as soon as her mother settled down to study. Rufus went with her, curled at the bottom of a brown paper bag in case they met Mr. Grady on the way. They found Molly in her kitchen, her usually paper-pale cheeks rosy. She smiled as she slid a batch of cookies onto a tray to cool.

"I hope you like lemon-drop cookies, Erin!" she cried. "And Rufus came, too! How nice! I woke up feeling stronger than usual this morning, and so I'm making the most of the day. We love lemon drops, don't we, darlings?"

"I certainly do." A doll in a red satin ball gown smiled down from the top of the refrigerator. "I could eat that whole trayful, I'm sure."

"Nice cat you have there." Erin turned to find the earl of Kirby propped against the breadbox at the end of the counter. "I prefer dogs myself, but a cat is a decent enough pet."

Rufus darted under the kitchen table and glared up at the earl with suspicion.

"Margaret Mary's in the bedroom closet, I'm sorry to say." Molly frowned briefly, and then her smile returned. "The silly girl wanted chocolate chip cookies when everyone else voted for lemon drops. I told her we'd do the chocolate chips next time, but she wouldn't listen. She's in a real rage about it—insisted on going into the closet where she won't have to talk to anyone. She's missing all the fun."

"Missing the cookies, too," the earl said. "Women!"

"Oh, don't act so superior," snapped the doll in red. "All women aren't like Margaret Mary, and you know it!"

"I'd like a cookie right now," the earl said calmly. "If it wouldn't be too much trouble."

Molly laid a lemon drop on his black-trousered knees. Then she sat down at the table and motioned Erin to sit, too. "You have a cookie, too, dear. I want to ask a favor. You mentioned the YWCA the other day."

"My mother keeps talking about it," Erin said grumpily. "She wants me to join, but I don't want to."

Molly just smiled. "Well, then you probably know the Y has a summer drama group. They're really very good—at least, they have been in the past. A week from Friday night is their first production of the season, but this year I don't dare venture out in the evening by myself. I've been wondering if you'd go with me. My treat, of course."

Erin stopped chewing. The melt-in-your-mouth cookie suddenly tasted like sawdust. She glanced at the earl and then at the smiling doll in red. They were both watching her with interested expressions. Rufus leaped up on her lap, and even he had a curiously expectant look.

"Well, I—" She didn't want anything to do with the Y and its summer drama group, but it was hard to say no to Molly Panca.

"I guess it'll be okay," she said finally. "I'll have to ask my mother."

Molly clapped her hands. "Oh, I do hope she'll let you go. It would be lovely to have a special night to look forward to."

Later, after more cookies, Molly took Erin into the bedroom to say hello to the rest of the family. Two of the dolls were at the window; the others sat in a circle on the bed with a deck of Old Maid cards in their midst. Molly went to the closet and opened the door a crack. She pointed to the top shelf where Margaret Mary lay, her face to the wall.

"Erin's here, dear. We're having cookies. Won't you join us?"

"I don't *like* lemon-drop cookies." Margaret Mary sounded as if she'd been crying. "If I can't have chocolate chips, I don't want any."

Erin retreated across the bedroom and scooped up Rufus. "I know you think I'm like Margaret Mary," she said accusingly. "You make her say those dumb things so I'll feel stupid. But I don't care! Why should I pretend I'm having a good time this summer when I'm not?"

"I don't think anyone should have to pretend to be happy," Molly said seriously. "But I do wish Margaret Mary would *try* to enjoy life." She closed the closet door and followed Erin into the living room. "The truth is," she whispered, "Margaret Mary is my favorite. You've never seen her at her best, Erin. She's a darling when she isn't feeling sorry for herself. Please don't forget about the play, dear. It's based on a wonderful book. You'll enjoy it."

Erin dropped Rufus into the paper bag and cradled the bag in her arms. She was already trying to think of a way to get out of taking Molly to the play.

"Maybe you've read the book," Molly continued. "It's always been one of my favorites—*A Little Princess*. Have you heard of it?"

Erin gulped. "I've read it," she said in a strangled voice.

"And do you like it?"

"I used to," Erin admitted. She opened the door. "But not anymore. That Sara Crewe is too good to be true." She fled down the hall, squeezing the bag so hard that Rufus meowed in protest.

Chapter Thirteen

"We played your video five times! My mom and dad watched it, too. We all think you and your family are terrific actors. Maybe you can write another one this fall with parts for Meg and Emily and me.

"You say Milwaukee is dull, but it doesn't sound dull. Emily says she would give ten million dollars to see the talking dolls. And Meg says you must be sure to go to a seance before you come home. Do you think your mother will let you?"

Erin put down Heather's letter and leaned out of the living room window to watch her father and Cowper. They were in the narrow side yard, tossing a softball slowly back and forth. It was what they did every afternoon now when Cowper finished his practice session at the conservatory. At first her father had tried to get Erin to join them, but after she'd refused a few times, he'd stopped asking. It would be boring, she told herself. When she and her father played catch, the ball shot crisply back and forth, but when Cowper was part of the game you had to remember that his hands might be hurt by a fast-flying ball.

"Have to give our boy a little exercise," Mr. Lindsay said. "He hasn't had a chance to make any friends his own age around here."

"What about me?" Erin wanted to ask, but she kept still. She knew what the answer would be, and she didn't want to hear it: "You could meet people if you tried, old girl. Get busy!"

Back and forth, back and forth the ball swooped, the rhythm broken only when Cowper missed a catch. Erin watched a few minutes longer, until Rufus leaped up on the couch beside her.

"What a pretty boy you are!" She leaned back and ran her fingers over the golden coat. It reminded her of the Bengal tigers she'd seen at the zoo last Saturday.

The zoo, when they finally got there, had been wonderful. For a whole afternoon Erin had relaxed and forgotten how angry she was with Cowbird. The Lindsays strolled contentedly from the elephants to the tigers to the monkeys and the penguins.

They picnicked in a sunny corner and ended the day riding on the little train that circled the park. It wasn't until the car turned onto Kirby Avenue and the apartment building loomed into sight that Erin felt her dark, sad self come stealing back.

"I wish we didn't have to go in," she said. "I wish this afternoon could go on forever."

Mrs. Lindsay, her nose burned red, gave Erin a hug. "I wish it could go on, too," she said. "But we'll do other fun things, I promise. Maybe the museum next weekend. Or a movie, if we can find a good one."

Erin nodded. *A whole week away*, she thought.

"You have the play to look forward to on Friday," her mother had added cheerfully. "It was sweet of Miss Panca to invite you."

That had been nearly a week ago. Now, leaning back on the couch with Rufus in her arms, Erin thought about how much she *didn't* want to see *A Little Princess*. Once she would have been thrilled at the thought of watching Sara Crewe come to life; now she wished she could forget the book that had once been her favorite. Sara was a perfect person. She and Sara were nothing alike, and they never would be.

At supper Erin's mother announced that Mr. Salzman had sent a note asking the Lindsays to come to see him. Even though Cowper had failed the audition, the instructor was pleased with his youngest student's progress and wanted to talk about plans for his future. Mr. and Mrs. Lindsay could hardly wait for the Thursday evening conference.

"I told you there was no reason to be discouraged,

Cowper," Mrs. Lindsay said gaily. "We're so proud of you!"

"I hope you're proud of yourself," Erin's father added. "All this hard work is paying off, isn't it?"

"Yup." Cowper stared grimly into space. But it didn't matter whether he showed any enthusiasm. Erin's parents were convinced that he loved what he was doing. They were happy with him just the way he was.

There was nothing interesting on television early in the evening. If there had been, Erin thought later, her whole life might have turned out differently.

She wouldn't have gone looking for Rufus.

She wouldn't have wandered into Cowbird's room and discovered his window standing open.

She wouldn't have leaned out into the twilight just in time to see a red-gold tail vanishing around the ledge at the rear of the building.

"Rufus!" She barely whispered his name, too horrified to scream.

Suddenly Cowper was there beside her, leaning out the window. "It's okay," he said. "No big deal." He went back and closed the door to the hallway.

"But where did he go?" Erin couldn't move. She could only stare at the corner where her cat had disappeared.

"Don't worry about him," Cowper said. "He's just

gone out for some fresh air. I do it all the time. Watch."
He swung his legs over the windowsill and stood there
facing the wall. Then he edged along the ledge and
vanished around the corner, just as Rufus had.

Erin felt as if she had stepped into a nightmare. She
clutched the sill with trembling fingers. After a moment a small hand appeared at the corner, the thumb
and third finger touching in an "everything's okay"
signal. Then Cowper's head came into sight, and he
gave her one of his rare smiles.

"Your cat's coming," he said, as if it were the most
ordinary thing in the world to walk along an eighteen-
inch-wide ledge five stories above the ground. Erin
held her breath as Cowper moved sideways toward her,
his hands pressed against the wall. It wasn't until he
was inside the bedroom that she dared to speak.

"Where—"

"I told you." Cowper brushed off his knees. "He's
sitting out there on the porch. It's neat."

"What porch?" Erin demanded. She leaned out again
and stared at the empty ledge.

"You know—at the end of the hall. Behind that
sealed-up door."

Erin stared at him. She'd forgotten all about the door
hidden by the chest of drawers at the end of the hallway. "But that's not a *real* porch," she protested. "I
thought—"

Cowper leaned against the dresser, his hands in his

pockets. "Sure it's a real porch," he said patiently. "It just doesn't have any railings. The people who built this place about a million years ago ran out of money— I told you, remember?—and they decided not to finish the porches. They sealed up the door at the end of the hall. But you can still sit out there—if you don't mind the walk and the jump. You have to jump from the ledge to the porch."

Erin felt sick. "I want Rufus to come back," she moaned, trying not to cry. "He could be killed!"

At that moment the big cat strolled around the corner. His tail was high, and he seemed completely at ease as he dawdled along the ledge. Two or three feet from the window he sat down and licked his front paws thoughtfully. Then he stood up, stretched, and in a single leap he landed on the sill. Erin grabbed him and pulled him inside, slamming the window shut with the other hand.

"Oh, Ruf." She cradled the cat in her arms. "How could you do such a terrible thing?"

"Don't blame him," Cowper said. "I forgot to close the screen last time I came in."

For the first time Erin took in the full meaning of what Cowper was saying. He'd been out there before— lots of times!

"But you can't do that!" she protested. "You mustn't! It's the dumbest thing I ever heard of!"

Cowper's jaw tightened. "I can if I want to," he

said. "I like sitting out there. I can think about stuff."

"What stuff?"

"Just stuff. I even slept out on the porch one night. It was great—like floating. Just because you'd be afraid to do it . . ."

Erin gripped Rufus more firmly. "I wouldn't be afraid," she lied. Nothing could make her climb out on the narrow ledge. "And I'm going to tell Mom and Dad what you're doing. You'll be grounded forever."

It occurred to her as she said it that grounding wouldn't matter much to Cowper. He never went anywhere except to the conservatory. He never did anything except play the piano.

"Don't tell." Maybe he didn't care about being grounded, but he did sound worried.

Erin stalked out of the room. Minutes later, with Rufus safely shut up in her own room, she tiptoed down the hall, hoping to slip out of the apartment without being seen.

"Is that you, Erin? Where are you going?" Her mother was in the living room, out of sight but not out of earshot.

Erin hesitated. "Downstairs," she said finally. "I won't be gone long."

"I hope you aren't making a pest of yourself," Mrs. Lindsay said. "Your friend Molly may not be ready for company whenever the mood strikes you."

"I said I'll be right back." Erin let herself out and closed the door quickly. She wasn't going to visit Molly Panca.

Silvery evening light softened Kirby Avenue and gave it a mysterious look. Erin hurried down the front steps and around the side of the building to the yard where her father and Cowper had been playing ball a couple of hours before. At the far end of the strip of lawn, a row of dumpsters loomed like dinosaurs. She squeezed between two of them, into the paved back-yard and looked up at the back of the building.

The porches that were not really porches went up the back wall in two rows, like the rungs of ladders. Each porch was a tiny platform without railings, held in place by frail-looking braces. The ledges, beginning on the sides of the building and continuing around the back, came to an end a couple of feet or more from each porch.

You have to jump. When Cowper went out there, he jumped from the ledge to the porch over five stories of empty space.

He could kill himself, Erin thought. *If he fell, or if the porch gave way while he was on it, he'd be gone.*

Cowper would be gone.

For a moment, Erin couldn't breathe.

Chapter Fourteen

There was spaghetti for dinner—Erin's favorite. Usually she had two helpings, but tonight she could hardly swallow a bite. Cowper's secret was in the way, like a lump in her throat.

She had to tell her parents he was sneaking out on the porch. Cowper would call her a tattletale, but it wasn't tattling when you told for a good reason. She couldn't let him go on doing such a dangerous thing.

Could she?

"You're awfully quiet tonight. Cat got your tongue, my queen?"

Erin looked up guiltily, then returned to pushing her spaghetti around the plate.

"Penny for your thoughts," her father persisted. "No, make that a nickel. You look as if you're carrying quite a load."

Across the table, Cowper put down his fork and took

a deep breath. *Now*, Erin thought. *Now I'll tell them.*

She shook her head. "It's nothing," she said faintly. "I was just thinking."

Mrs. Lindsay made a little face. "Thinking or moping?" she asked. "I've forgotten what your smile looks like, Erin. The last time I saw it was—let me see—when we were making the video. What did you do today, anyway?"

"Watched TV," Erin replied. "Wrote a letter to Meg. Washed my hair." *And found out Cowper's practically committing suicide.* She pushed the thought away and looked at her mother defiantly. "What's wrong with writing letters and washing my hair?"

"Nothing's *wrong* with it. You just sound like a little old lady, that's all. You need some exercise, for goodness' sake. Some variety. You need to get out of this apartment." She frowned. "There must be someplace around here where you can use your skateboard. All the sidewalks can't be as bad as they are in front of this building."

"They are," Erin said. "I've looked."

"She's right. The walks are pretty much messed up for blocks around," her father said. "I don't think she should try it. Besides," he added, "skateboarding on city sidewalks isn't such a great idea. There may even be a law against it."

"Well," Mrs. Lindsay sounded exasperated, "there

has to be something she can do besides sit around feeling sorry for herself. If she won't give the Y a chance . . ."

Erin thought of Margaret Mary sulking on the top shelf of Molly Panca's closet. She hadn't been back to visit Molly for several days. Tomorrow was Friday, the night they were to go see *A Little Princess*. Now, more than ever, Erin didn't want to go. Perfect Sara Crewe would certainly have told her parents at once if she'd discovered that her foster brother was risking his life.

Well, I'm just not a goody-goody like Sara, she thought. *Cowbird's only three years younger than I am. He knows what he's doing. It's not my fault if he acts crazy. It's not my fault if he gets himself killed.*

For the last couple of hours Erin had been trying to imagine what life would be like if there were no Cowbird. Now she let herself think about it again. Her mother and father would be sad for a while. *I might be sad, too. For a while.* But then they would go back to Clinton, and everything would be the way it had been before Cowbird came to live with them. Erin could no longer remember exactly what that had been like, but she was sure she had had more fun—and more attention—than she had now. They would be a normal family again, without a genius child who had to be pampered and followed around the country wherever his piano playing took him.

"Erin, what in the world is the matter with you? You're absolutely white!"

Erin jumped, startled by her mother's question. They were all looking at her, as if they could actually see the wicked thoughts crowding her brain.

"Nothing's the matter!" she exclaimed. "I'm okay. I'm fine." But then, as clearly as if it had already happened, Erin pictured Cowbird falling through the air. Saw him lying on the pavement behind the apartment. With a gasp she leaped up from the table and ran down the hall to the bathroom, barely making it before the spaghetti came back up.

Her mother followed her. "What's wrong? Are you coming down with the flu?" She pressed a cool hand to Erin's forehead. "What's bothering you, hon?"

Erin leaned against the bathtub and closed her eyes, shutting out her mother's anxious face. "I'm all right— my stomach's just upset."

"Are you sure?"

Erin nodded. "I'm sure I don't have the flu." She kept her eyes closed till she heard her mother sigh and go back down the hall.

"I wish you'd come with us tonight."

Mrs. Lindsay stood in the doorway of Erin's room, looking worried. She was wearing her best red-and-gold print dress and her big gold earrings for the interview with Cowper's Mr. Salzman. "You still haven't seen the conservatory," she coaxed. "And besides, I don't like leaving you home alone, especially when you don't feel well."

"I don't mind being alone," Erin said. She was curled up on the studio couch with Rufus at her feet. "I just want to lie here for a while." *And go to sleep*, she added to herself. If she slept, she could stop thinking about the ledge, stop seeing Cowper walking on it, falling from it.

"I don't know," Mrs. Lindsay said doubtfully. "Maybe one of us should stay home."

"Are you ready?" Mr. Lindsay called from the front hall. "We have less than twenty minutes to get there."

Mrs. Lindsay sighed. She hurried across the room and bent to kiss Erin's cheek. "I suppose it'll be all right," she said. "You just rest, dear. We'll be back before you know it."

Erin pressed her face into the pillow and closed her eyes. She took deep breaths and tried to empty her mind. *Go to sleep*.

It didn't work. After a few minutes she sat up and reached for Rufus. He had moved to the windowsill and was staring longingly through the screen at the ledge below.

"Oh no, you don't." Erin went to the window and gathered him in her arms. A storm was building in the west, sending long fingers of lightning across the sky. Erin watched, flinching as the flashes of light came closer and the first drops of rain splattered against the screen.

Back in Clinton, Erin had always enjoyed storms. From her bedroom window she could watch the swaying branches of the oak tree and the streaming yellow-green "hair" of the giant willows. When lightning flared over the bluffs along the river, it was a beautiful sight, like fireworks. But on Kirby Avenue, the harsh flashes lit up nothing but ugliness.

Now Rufus noticed the lightning and pushed his head under her arm. Erin wandered down the hall to Cowper's bedroom and stared out at the ledge. It was slippery-looking in the pelting rain.

What Cowbird does is none of your business. Why should you care? The harsh voice inside her head refused to be still.

"I *don't* care," she said out loud. "It's not my fault if something awful happens to him."

Of course it's not your fault. Nobody can blame you if he takes stupid chances. . . .

If only Heather or Meg were close by, they would help her think about something else. If only . . . But what was the use of wishing? There was no one around to talk to but Molly Panca, and Molly was more like a sweet old aunt than a best friend. Besides, she already knew what Molly would say: "You must love your brother and do what's best for him, the poor little tyke."

It was easy enough to talk about loving if the only people you had to put up with were dolls.

"*Meow!*" Another bolt of lightning, startlingly close, sent Rufus hurtling out of Erin's arms and under the bed. She bent to coax him out, just as a crash of thunder made the apartment tremble. The lights flickered and went off.

For a moment Erin was too startled to move. Then she stumbled across the bedroom and out into the hall. Where had they put the flashlight when they unpacked the boxes? She pressed against the wall and made her way into the kitchen. The top drawer of the cupboard was her mother's you-name-it-we-have-it place.

A moment later Erin had the flashlight in her hand. The thin beam of light sliced through the darkness, guiding her to the foyer. But when she opened the apartment door a crack and peered out, the hall was as black as the rooms behind her. The whole building must be without power.

Now what? Erin tried not to panic. She could stay in the apartment, but her family wouldn't be home for a couple of hours. What if the flashlight battery wore out before then? Or she could go down to Molly Panca's apartment right now, while she still had a light to help her find her way. She didn't want to do either, but of the two possibilities, going to see Molly sounded better. They could eat cookies and talk with the dolls (except Margaret Mary, who would probably be pouting, as usual).

Erin opened the door and pointed the thin pencil of light toward the back stairs. Darkness and her own nervousness transformed the hall into a terrifying tunnel.

When she reached 405, the door was open a crack.

"Molly?" She couldn't keep a quiver out of her voice. "Is it okay if I come in?"

The voice that answered was not Molly Panca's. "Sounds like that girl who broke into my apartment while I was sleeping. What's she want?"

Mr. Barnhart! Erin backed away. She didn't feel like being teased.

"Erin, is that you?" The door opened the rest of the way, and Molly smiled out at her, a candle in one hand. She wore a bright red blouse with a huge bow knotted under her chin, and there was a matching red ribbon tied around her white curls.

"I just came to visit," Erin said. "The lights went out and I—" She paused. "My mom and dad are at Cowper's school—"

"You mean you're home alone? Oh, my dear." Molly touched her arm lightly. "You poor child. Come right in."

Erin didn't move. "You have company—"

"Dear friends," Molly corrected her. "They've come for a seance, you see. We were just about to start when the lights went, and I had to stop and hunt for more candles."

"A seance? You're having a seance right now?"

"Oh my!" Molly looked unhappy. "What am I thinking of? I can't let you stay without your parents' permission. It seems cruel to send you away, but—"

"Please!" Erin couldn't bear to go back upstairs to the dark, empty apartment. "My mom and dad won't mind," she insisted. "They'll be glad I didn't have to stay alone in the dark."

"What's going on out there?" Mr. Barnhart called from the apartment. "When're we goin' to get this show on the road?"

Molly bit her lip. "I just don't know," she murmured, cringing at an especially loud crash of thunder. "Well . . ." She gave up. "I guess you can stay, dear. But you mustn't be frightened. We're all friends here, and the spirits are our friends, too. Do you understand?"

"I won't be afraid," Erin assured her. She followed Molly into the living room eagerly. Talking to ghosts would be scary, but she liked being scared. And whatever happened, it would be a hundred times better than sitting all alone in the dark, with nothing to keep her company but the painful thoughts of the last few hours.

Chapter Fifteen

Four people clustered around a card table in Molly Panca's tiny living room. Mr. Barnhart's fuzzy white hair shone like a halo in candlelight, and he grinned wickedly at Erin from under shaggy brows.

"There she is," he announced. "Best female fire-fighter in Milwaukee. Come to keep an eye on the candles, I s'pose."

Molly shook her finger at him. "Such a tease," she said fondly. "Erin, I'd like you to meet Miss Edith Brown, and this is her sister, Miss Cora Brown." Erin nodded at the ladies.

"We've met," Miss Cora Brown announced. "At the elevator one day. You'd been crying, as I remember."

"Crying!" Molly peered anxiously at Erin. "You're not crying now, are you, dear? Just a bit lonesome in the storm." She went back to her introductions. "This is Mrs. Grady. You've met *Mr.* Grady. He's the man who takes care of us all and keeps this building in such fine shape. And of course you know my family." She pointed at the row of dolls lined up on the sofa. "They look forward to the seances."

"We all do," Mr. Barnhart said dryly. "But it don't usually take this long to get one started."

Molly smiled cheerfully. "Erin's going to join us this evening, so we'll need one more minute to get her settled. I'm afraid you'll have to use the kitchen stool, dear. If you don't mind."

Erin hurried out to the kitchen, grateful to escape Mrs. Grady's hard stare and the Brown sisters' curious examination. *Good thing I didn't stop to pick up Rufus before I came down here*, she thought. Mrs. Grady looked as if she'd disapprove of pets as much as her husband did.

When Erin returned to the living room, Molly was seated at the card table beside Mrs. Grady.

"You can sit over here next to me," Mr. Barnhart said, moving his chair to one side. "Jest put your fingertips on the table—like you was playing the piano—and watch what happens."

Erin obeyed, her heart thumping with excitement. On her other side, Molly Panca leaned back in her chair with her eyes closed. She had put her candlestick on the bookshelf behind her, and the bright little flame quivered and danced above her curls.

"Now we're ready to meet our spirit friends," she said softly. "Tell us, spirits, if you are with us. Let the table tell us." She began to move her fingers in wide circles over the tabletop.

There was a long silence, in which the smell of incense seemed to grow stronger. Erin looked at the Brown sisters, both of whom had their eyes closed, and at Mr. Barnhart, who had pretended to close his eyes but was peeking. Mrs. Grady's eyes were wide open. She stared fiercely at the table, as if daring it to tell her anything.

Erin felt the hair rise across the back of her neck. She was sure the table had moved, a tiny but unmistakable shift.

"There she goes," Mr. Barnhart whispered gleefully. "What'd I tell ya!"

"Emma Barnhart, are you with us this evening?" Molly Panca spoke in a low, robot voice, completely unlike her own. As if in answer, the battered old card table began to rise, shakily, under their fingertips. For a second it hovered. Then it dropped down again, and two loud knocks sounded from beneath it.

"Two means yes," Mr. Barnhart explained in a pleased whisper. "Emma's here, bless her. Never missed yet, have ya, old girl?"

"Don't say 'old girl.' " Mrs. Grady looked offended. "It doesn't sound respectful."

Mr. Barnhart winked at Erin. "I called my Emma 'old girl' when she was alive. Can't see any reason to do different now. Molly, you goin' to ask her what I told you?"

Molly's face was still. "Emma dear," she said in the same soft, faraway voice, "John wants to know whether he should go to Chicago to live with your children when we have to leave this building. What do you think?"

Erin held her breath. A single sharp rap came from beneath the table.

"I knew it!" Mr. Barnhart looked around triumphantly. "I knew she'd say no. We never did like to depend on our kids for things. Emma wants me to find a new place here in town. Right, old girl?"

"Well," Miss Edith Brown snapped, "if you already knew that's what you were planning, I don't see why you took up everybody's time asking. You can put your name in for an apartment in that new low-income place, same as the rest of us."

Mr. Barnhart smiled at her. "That's right," he agreed. "But I wouldn't do it without askin' my Emma."

During this discussion, Molly Panca's eyes remained closed; she'd have seemed asleep if it weren't for those constantly moving fingertips. She looked, Erin decided, exactly the way a medium ought to look. And the shadowy living room, the soft candlelight, the crashes of thunder were spooky and *right*. It was the people around the table who were strangely out of tune with the occasion. Spirits and rappings and the mysteriously moving table didn't startle Molly's visitors in the least.

"It's our turn now," Edith Brown said. "Is Father here?" The sisters leaned forward expectantly and looked at each other with relief as two raps sounded from under the table.

"Quick, Molly. Ask him if we should sell the Chinese vase and use the money to go to Florida this winter," Cora said with a defiant glance at her sister. "I'm sure that's what he'll want us to do."

"He won't!" Edith Brown retorted. "That vase has been in the family for ages."

"Oh, for goodness' sake!" Mrs. Grady exclaimed. "Why don't you just—"

The table rocked sharply, cutting short Mrs. Grady's advice.

"Cora and Edith would like your opinion, dear spirit," Molly murmured. "Do you think they should sell the Chinese vase and go to Florida this winter?"

Silence.

"He's disgusted with us for even suggesting it." Edith sounded panicky. "I warned you."

Cora pressed her lips together.

"Please tell us," Molly begged. "Do you think Cora and Edith should go to Florida this winter, spirit?"

This time the two raps came quickly. Cora Brown gave a crow of delight.

"Yes! That means we're going!" she chortled. "Oh, I'm so happy!"

Edith glared at her sister and then at Molly. "There must be a mistake," she said fiercely. "He never wanted to part with that vase."

"Well, he wants to now," Mr. Barnhart interrupted briskly. "You can't argue with the spirits, old girl."

Edith Brown sniffed. She looked around the little living room as if she'd gladly argue if she could see someone to argue with.

"Let's get on with this," Mrs. Grady said impatiently. "It's my turn, Miss Panca. And please don't expect me to be satisfied with raps and table rocking. That's all very well for *some* questions, I'm sure, but my problem is important. Life and death, you might say. I want to talk to Cousin Caroline myself, if you please."

Edith Brown sniffed. "As if a rare old Chinese vase isn't important."

Mrs. Grady ignored her. "It's Cousin Caroline's daughter I'm worried sick about. Caroline *must* tell me what she wants me to do!"

Erin fought down an uneasy giggle. Mrs. Grady

sounded as if she expected people—and spirits—to move fast when she gave orders.

"We will try to talk to Cousin Caroline," Molly Panca said softly. "I can't promise she'll speak, but we'll try. Please be very quiet, everyone. . . . Cousin Caroline, are you with us?"

The Brown sisters stopped scowling at each other, and Mr. Barnhart nodded proudly. "Molly will bring 'er in," he whispered to Erin. "You just wait."

"Let us know if you are with us, Cousin Caroline," Molly pleaded. "Mrs. Grady longs to hear from you."

The answer made them all gasp. "I am here." A woman's voice spoke clearly from the bedroom. "What is it you want?"

"For heaven's sake!" Mrs. Grady stared with narrowed eyes into the darkness of the bedroom. "I don't see her," she said. "Where is she?"

Cora Brown gave a little whimper. "Oh, don't make us *see* her," she begged. "I don't want to *see* a ghost."

"I am here," the voice repeated. "What do you wish to know?"

Mrs. Grady patted her forehead with a large plaid handkerchief. "Well, if that's really you, Caroline," she said, sounding nervous for the first time, "I want to know what to do about that daughter of yours. You asked me to keep an eye on her when she came to Milwaukee to work, but I never dreamed you were going to up and die. And I didn't know she was going to get engaged. Caroline, he's a terrible man. He treats her badly. And he has dirty fingernails. What should I do?"

They had all turned in their chairs to peer into the dark bedroom—all except Molly who still had her eyes closed and a peaceful expression on her white face.

"What would you do if you were here, Caroline?" Mrs. Grady was beginning to sound more like her impatient self. "Don't just hide there in the dark—speak up."

Erin could hardly believe her ears. Mrs. Grady was scolding a spirit! *Just the way she probably scolds Cousin Caroline's poor daughter*, she thought.

"If I could talk to her," said the voice in the bedroom, "I'd tell her I love her."

"Love her!" Mrs. Grady was highly annoyed. "What's that got to do with anything? I asked you what to do about her wretched boyfriend."

"She's so lonely in the city," the voice said. "She needs somebody. She may not be thinking very clearly right now, but it would help if she knew you cared."

"Well, of course I care," Mrs. Grady snapped. "But I don't see—"

"Tell her you love her," the voice repeated, fainter now. "Tell her, and see what happens."

"Well, I never!" Mrs. Grady exclaimed in the silence that followed. "What kind of advice is that?"

"Sounded good to me," Mr. Barnhart said. "Wish I'd told my Emma I loved her more often when I had the chance. What do you think, girl?"

"I—I don't know." Erin shrank from Mrs. Grady's outraged glare.

"Of course she doesn't know!" Mrs. Grady exclaimed. "Neither do I. What good does it do to say 'I love you'?"

"I think it's a very nice idea," Miss Cora Brown announced bravely. She looked at her sister. "I believe it would help *me* to think more clearly if someone said it to *me* once in a while."

For some reason, Erin thought of Cowper and the strange lost look he wore much of the time. But Cowper had Erin's parents to tell him they loved him; there was no reason for him to feel lonely. Unless—unless he thought it was just his piano playing they loved!

"Now it's the girl's turn." Mr. Barnhart broke in on Erin's disturbing thoughts. "You have a question for the spirits, girl?"

"N-no!" Suddenly, Erin had seen enough of the seance. She pushed herself back from the table and was starting to get up, when Molly Panca spoke in her robot voice.

"There is another spirit present. There is another message. I believe it's for—"

"—for the pretty little girl there with you." They all

peered into the bedroom, trying to find the source of this new voice. "She is very unhappy."

"Unhappy?" Mr. Barnhart repeated. "What've you got to be unhappy about, girl? And who's the spirit that's talkin' to ya?"

Erin sat down hard. "I don't know," she gasped. "I don't know who that is." And yet the voice had been oddly familiar.

"You must make good things happen," it continued. "Do it now. There's no time to waste."

Erin stared hard at Molly Panca's still face. It had to be Molly talking; she was always telling Margaret Mary to enjoy life instead of complaining. And yet when she looked back at the bedroom door, for a second or two she thought she saw a looming shape, a shadow darker than the darkness around it.

"Help yourself, Erin," the voice intoned, becoming fainter. "And help your little brother. . . ."

Erin snatched up the flashlight from the floor beside her and jumped to her feet. "I have to go home!" she exclaimed. "Honestly! If my mom and dad come back, they'll be worried. I have to go right now!"

She ran to the door, desperate to get away before the voice said more. Whoever it was, Molly or a spirit, it knew too much, understood too much.

When Erin looked back from the door, Molly Panca's bright blue eyes were open and watching. Erin lunged out into the hall, the flashlight beam bobbing through the blackness.

"Don't run in the halls, young lady." Mrs. Grady's harsh cry followed her. "You'll knock someone down, and we'll have a lawsuit on our hands."

Erin ignored the warning. She felt as if some terrible, all-knowing phantom were about to clutch her arm and pronounce judgment.

You are an evil person, Erin Lindsay. Only a really bad person would want to get rid of her little brother.

As she pushed the key into her apartment door, the lights went on. Erin leaned, trembling, against the door and looked up and down the hall.

Empty.

She took a long, shuddering breath and let herself into her apartment. Rufus was waiting just inside the door, lying on the floor, his front paws crossed and his tail flicking. He reminded her of—of—and suddenly she knew why the second spirit voice had sounded familiar. It really had been a voice she had heard before.

The thin, whiny voice of the stone lion.

Chapter Sixteen

"Well, I suppose it was good of her to take you in under the circumstances," Mrs. Lindsay said. "But I just don't like the idea of your attending a seance, Erin."

"What happened?" Cowper wanted to know. "Does she really talk to dead people?"

"No, she doesn't," Erin's father answered for her. "It sounds to me as if Molly Panca is a good lady with lots of smarts and a great sense of drama. She wants to help her friends make difficult decisions, and she knows they'll pay more attention to spirits than to her. She's an expert ventriloquist, so it can't be hard for her to come up with a spirit voice or two. And it probably isn't so hard to make a table hop once you know the trick."

"Still, I'm sure you'll have nightmares tonight," Mrs. Lindsay insisted.

"No, I won't," Erin said. "I think Daddy's right about Molly—she was making the table move. The whole seance was hardly scary at all." (*Except for the last part*! She hadn't told them there'd been a message for Erin Lindsay.)

"Well, I think that's rotten!" Cowper exclaimed. He looked fiercely disappointed. "I don't see how you can call her good if she's fooling people all the time."

"She *is* good," Erin retorted, just as fiercely. "Molly's trying to make people happy. What's bad about that?"

She didn't have nightmares, but Erin did have a hard time getting to sleep that night. She wished she hadn't stayed for the seance. How she felt about Cowbird was no one else's business. She didn't have to love him, or help him, if she didn't want to. But somehow, Molly knew people's real thoughts. That was frightening. In spite of what Erin had said to Cowper at dinner, she wasn't sure she liked Molly Panca anymore.

At least she didn't have to wonder whether Cowbird was sleeping out on the porch tonight. The rain beating briskly on his bedroom window would keep him inside. He might not worry about falling five stories, but he hated getting wet.

The next day seemed endless, with the play looming unpleasantly at the end of it. Halfway through the morning Erin went out to the kitchen where her father had his books and papers spread out on the table.

"What's the matter? Nothing to do?" He ran a hand through his hair and scowled at the notes in front of him. "What's on your mind?"

Erin shrugged. She could tell him about Cowper and the ledge now. Get it over with. If she wanted to. ("You mean you've known this since yesterday afternoon, and you haven't said anything till now? Why not, Erin? What kind of person are you?")

"I never should have taken economics," Mr. Lindsay muttered. "It's killing me." He rubbed his forehead and waited for her to say something. "Problems?"

Erin shook her head. "I just—wondered what you were doing."

He made a face. "What I'm doing is making myself sick. I feel as if I were ten years old and about to flunk a spelling test. I'm sorry, but I guess I'm not in a chatty mood."

Erin retreated to the living room and curled up with a book of ghost stories. An hour later, when her mother came home from the university, Erin followed her into her bedroom.

"There's something I should probably tell you," she began cautiously.

Her mother's lips tightened. "If it's about the play

tonight, please don't start again, Erin. You *can't* disappoint Miss Panca. She's been a good friend to you, and I'm sure she's looking forward to this tremendously. I really don't understand why you don't want to go."

Erin bit her lip. "It isn't that."

"If you're worried about getting to the Y and home again, don't be. Your dad is going to take you and pick you up. So you see, you're a lucky girl with nothing to complain about. We should all be feeling great—especially now, with Mr. Salzman so pleased with Cowper's progress." Her face changed, glowed with pleasure. "He told us last night that Cowper's problem at the audition doesn't mean a thing. He thinks there's no limit to what he'll accomplish in the future. Isn't that marvelous?"

Erin nodded and went back to the living room, her stomach churning.

When her father and Cowper came home, late in the afternoon, Erin watched again from the window as they played ball in the yard next to the apartment building. Beyond the grassy plot, the bulldozer crawled back and forth across the next lot, pushing and smoothing the rubble there. A siren sounded distantly, came closer. Its wail suited Erin's mood.

After dinner she went to her room to change from jeans to clean blue slacks and her favorite bright-red top. Then she lay down on the studio couch and stared at the ceiling, waiting for seven o'clock. Nothing could save her now from a whole evening of Sara Crewe's perfection.

At a few minutes before seven, there was a knock on her door. Cowbird peered in. He looked like a little old man, Erin thought, so solemn and pale. His eyes seemed bigger than ever behind the thick glasses.

"Thanks for not telling," he said in his slow way. "About the ledge. I thought you were going to."

Erin sat up. "I still might," she said coldly. "You're crazy to go out there. Really crazy."

Cowper blinked. "What do you care?" he asked, and from the way he stood there, waiting, it seemed that he really expected Erin to answer.

"What I don't see," she said finally, "is how you can do a crazy thing like that, and yet not tell my mom and dad how you really feel about playing the piano."

"That's different," he said and backed out of the room.

Erin lay down again, wishing she could call back her words. The look on his face had reminded her of the little lost puppy that had shown up in front of their house last winter. She reminded herself that Cowbird was to blame for that unhappy memory, too. If it weren't for him, her father might have let her keep the pup. Instead, he'd taken it to the Humane Society the very next day. ("We'll be in Milwaukee all next summer, my queen. Who's going to take care of him then? And what about the summer after that? Who knows where we'll be!")

Erin looked at her watch and saw that it was seven o'clock. If it weren't for Cowbird, she'd be in Clinton right now, having pizza with her friends or getting ready to go to the movies. If it weren't for Cowbird . . .

"Erin." Her father leaned into the room. "Are you ready? You go downstairs and pick up Miss Panca. I'll meet you both at the front door with the car at seven fifteen."

"Okay." Erin dragged herself up and brushed her hair. *Might as well get it over with*, she thought. *But I'd do anything to get out of this. Out of this evening. Out of this whole summer!*

Erin gave Rufus a farewell pat and said good-bye to her mother in the living room. Outside, the long hallway was stuffy and smelled, as usual, of somebody's dinner. Erin went slowly down the back stairs, making the walk to Molly's apartment last as long as possible.

She knocked and waited. Molly was probably arranging her "family" and thinking up another story about their day. Erin knocked again. The way she felt now, she might tell Molly, right out, that she didn't believe in talking dolls. Or talking stone lions. Or talking ghosts. It was all silliness! Had anyone ever said things like that to Molly Panca? Probably not. Erin thought of how Molly's smile would disappear and the sparkle would fade from her blue eyes and Erin knew she wouldn't say those words, either.

There was no sound inside 405. Erin turned the doorknob, but the door was locked. That was strange. Molly never locked her door during the day. She said she had nothing worth stealing, and she wanted to be sure her friends could come in whenever they wished. Why didn't Molly answer? She'd been looking forward to this evening and had probably been dressed and ready to go since lunchtime.

A door opened down the hall, and a bent figure came out. At first Erin didn't recognize Mr. Barnhart. She'd never thought of him as small, but in the half-light of the hallway, he looked very frail.

"Who's that?" he called. "Who's knockin' at Molly's door?"

"It's Erin." More uneasy than ever, Erin started down the hall toward him. "Do you know where she is?" she asked. "We're supposed to go to a play together."

She was close enough now to see that Mr. Barnhart's halo of white hair was tousled, and his eyes were red.

"Well, you can't go to no play with her now," he

said gruffly. "Can't do anything else, either. She's gone."

"Gone?" Erin stared at the old man. "She was supposed to wait for me. We were going together."

"I said she's *gone*," Mr. Barnhart repeated sharply. His expression changed as he realized Erin didn't understand what he was talking about. "Don't you know what *gone* is, girl? Our Molly's gone, same as my Emma. It's terrible!"

Erin stared at him. "You mean she'd *dead*? But she can't be dead. We were here just last night—"

"Had a heart attack this afternoon," Mr. Barnhart muttered. "You know how sick she was—never far from goin', if the truth be told. And now we've lost her." He looked at Erin with pain-filled eyes. "Didn't you hear the siren? Ambulance come and took her away. Died in the hospital."

"I didn't know she was sick," Erin said. She still couldn't believe what Mr. Barnhart was saying. "She never told me." But even as she said it, scraps of Molly's talk rattled around in her head—"It's too late for some of us, but Margaret Mary is young and strong. . . ."

"All you had to do was look at her," Mr. Barnhart said. "A person could tell how sickly she was."

"Thanks—thanks for telling me," Erin said shakily. She backed away from Mr. Barnhart, then turned and fled down the hall to the stairs. His cracked voice followed her.

"Goin' to miss her—all of us. She kept us in touch. Kept us on the straight and narrow."

Erin didn't stop running till she reached her own apartment. When she threw open the door, both of her parents were standing just inside. They turned to her with frightened faces.

"Something awful's happened!" Erin gasped. "Oh, Mom—"

Before she could go on, Mrs. Lindsay's hands flew up and she gave a little cry. "Erin, where is he?" she gasped. "Tell us!"

Erin swallowed the sob that threatened to choke her and looked from one of her parents to the other. What was her mother talking about?

"Cowper's disappeared," her father explained. "He went to his bedroom a while ago, but he's not there now. We didn't hear him leave, so he must have sneaked out. He knows he's not supposed to go out alone in the evenings—"

Erin darted past them down the hall to her foster brother's room. The window stood open. When she touched the screen, it flapped loosely.

"What are you doing?"

She hadn't realized her mother and father had followed her. Erin leaned out.

"Why look out there?" Mr. Lindsay demanded. "The boy can't fly."

Erin felt sick. "I—I think he might have gone out there," she stammered.

Before she could say more, there was a harsh, squawking noise, the sound of something breaking, tearing apart. It came from outside.

"What was that?" Mrs. Lindsay began to cry.

Erin's father pushed past her to look out at the ledge. "What was that noise, Erin? Do you know? What's going on?"

Erin hugged herself. She felt as if she might shatter into a thousand pieces. "Cowper's out there," she sobbed. "On the porch!"

"What are you talking about?" her father shouted. "There is no porch!"

The squawking sound came again—rusty bolts pulling loose from ancient brick. In the worst moment she'd ever known, Erin realized he was probably right. There was no porch.

Chapter Seventeen

"Around the back," Erin quavered. "Where the ledge ends. There was—is—a porch. You have to walk along the ledge and sort of jump—" She turned quickly from her mother's stricken look. "Cowper said there's a door in the hallway, Daddy, behind that chest of drawers. It's supposed to go to the porch, but it's closed up."

Mrs. Lindsay ran to the window and stared down at the ledge. "He *couldn't* walk on that!" she sobbed. "He couldn't! Oh, Cowper, come back here!"

Erin's father pulled her away from the window. "Don't call him, Grace. If he *is* out there, we don't want him walking along that ledge again, do we? I'll open the door and get him in that way." He gave Erin a stern look, a warning not to mention the noise they'd heard just moments ago.

They crowded back into the hallway and stared at the chest of drawers. Mr. Lindsay squeezed into the narrow space between the chest and the wall and braced himself.

"It's heavy!" he groaned. "Must weigh a ton!"

"Ken Krueger has it packed full of linens." Erin's mother pressed a hand against her mouth as if she were holding back screams. "Oh, hurry, please!"

Erin crouched and pulled the bottom drawer all the way out, letting it thump to the floor. She dragged it down the hall and hurried back to pull out the next one, stumbling over Rufus on the way.

"Smart girl!" Mr. Lindsay tried again and was able to shift the chest a few inches.

"Let me help," Mrs. Lindsay begged. She and Erin lifted out the third and fourth drawers together and were reaching for the next one when Mr. Lindsay motioned them away.

"That's enough. I can move it now."

One hard shove, then another, and the door behind the chest came into sight. Mr. Lindsay reached around and jerked the doorknob.

"Locked," he muttered. "Of course. Erin, get the toolkit on the top shelf of our bedroom closet. Hurry! I'll push the chest farther down the hall so there's room to work."

"You'll need an ax!" Mrs. Lindsay cried. "You'll have to break the door down!"

"No ax," Mr. Lindsay said grimly. "We don't know

what's on the other side. It might make things worse. . . ."

Erin ran down the hall. Her feet felt heavy, the way they did sometimes in dreams. She could hardly breathe. *Cowbird, I'm sorry.* . . . She had called him Cowbird, knowing that he hated it. She had been mean to him and cross and selfish, even when she knew he was unhappy. Now he was dead.

The toolkit was in the far corner of the closet shelf, out of reach. Erin dragged a chair across the floor and climbed up, teetering wildly before her stiff fingers closed around the vinyl case. When she ran back down the hall, her father had pushed the chest well out of the way and was crouched in front of the lock. He snatched the kit from Erin's trembling hands and set to work.

Erin and her mother watched. "I just don't see why he'd do such a thing," Mrs. Lindsay whispered over and over. "Are you sure—"

Erin shook her head. "Maybe he didn't," she said. "Maybe he went downstairs to take a walk, and you just didn't hear him leave." But she knew better. *He went out there, and I practically told him to go ahead and do it. I'll hate myself forever!*

She hadn't known it was possible to feel this bad.

"Get the flashlight," Mr. Lindsay snapped. "I can hardly see what I'm doing here."

Erin ran to the kitchen, grateful for another job.

When she returned, her father told her to stand behind him and hold the light over his shoulder. The doorknob was off. Working through the hole, he pushed the other knob out and then tried to release the bolt.

"Give me the smallest screwdriver! Quick!"

"I'll find it." Mrs. Lindsay snatched up the toolkit. "Maybe we should call Mr. Grady—"

There was a *click* from inside the door, and Mr. Lindsay gave a grunt of satisfaction.

"Got it! Now if the hinges aren't too rusted . . ." He hooked a finger into the hole left by the doorknob and pulled. "Have to go slow," he muttered. "Don't want to jar anything."

Mrs. Lindsay began to cry again, whimpery sounds Erin knew she would hear in her dreams forever. She felt like crying herself, but no tears came, even though her chest ached.

The door began to move under her father's steady pressure. When it was open a few inches, he stopped. His shoulders sagged, and he stepped back with a groan.

Erin leaned into the opening.

"Is he there?" Mrs. Lindsay demanded in a choked voice. "Tell me!" When no one answered, she pushed her way between Erin and Mr. Lindsay and stared through the opening with horror.

"Oh no!"

Erin tried to step back but couldn't. She wanted to run from the sight of the steeply tilted porch floor and the small brown pillow that was balanced on the high end. The pillow was one her mother had made for Cowper's room in Clinton, a needlepoint piano with musical notes floating around it.

"Get out of the way," Mr. Lindsay said hoarsely. "I'd better look. . . ."

He gripped the doorframe with one hand and leaned out, trying to see over the edge of the porch to the ground below.

"It's no use. I'll have to go downstairs—"

"I'm here."

For a second or two no one moved. Then they all turned together to stare at the sturdy little figure standing in the bedroom doorway.

"Cowper?" Mrs. Lindsay threw her arms around him. "Where did you come from? Where were you? Are you all right?"

Cowper stood stiffly, his face chalk white.

"I'm s-sorry if I scared you," he said shakily. "I didn't mean to."

"Scared us!" Mr. Lindsay shouted. "Scared us! I should think you did scare us! What were you thinking of, going out there like that."

Cowper took a step backward. "I won't do it again," he wailed. "Honest! I couldn't even if I wanted to. I slipped and fell on the ledge when I jumped from the porch just now. I must have kicked something loose. The dumb old porch is starting to fall down. I was shaking so hard I couldn't get up." He began to cry.

Erin watched dazedly as her parents comforted him. She could hardly believe that the nightmare was over and Cowper was alive. She hadn't killed him with her silence after all.

It took a while to get to The Question. First, Erin's parents wanted to know why Cowper had done a terrible, dangerous thing like walking on the ledge. There had to be a reason.

Cowper sank back into an overstuffed living room chair. "I thought about stuff out there," he said. It was the same answer he'd given Erin earlier.

"What kind of stuff?" Mrs. Lindsay demanded. "Did you think about playing the piano?"

"I thought about *not* playing. I thought about doing lots of other things."

"Like what?" Mr. Lindsay demanded.

Cowper sent a sidelong glance in Erin's direction. "Lots of things. Skateboarding, maybe. I told you that night at the restaurant. I'm not *good* at anything."

"But that's ridiculous!" Mrs. Lindsay was shocked. "You're good at—"

Erin's father looked thoughtful. "Besides playing the piano, you mean?"

Cowper nodded.

"Well, we'd better talk about that," Mr. Lindsay said. "You don't have to sit out in space to think about it all by yourself. We'll think about it together. I bet you'd be a good skateboarder. You just need some time to try."

"He might hurt his hands," Mrs. Lindsay protested. "I thought we settled all that. I thought you *wanted* to work hard and become a great pianist, Cowper. It's what your mother and father hoped would happen."

At the mention of his real parents, Cowper looked more unhappy than ever. "I know," he said despairingly. "I know that."

Erin braced herself. *Speak up*, the earl of Kirby had said. *It's the only way*. Margaret Mary had said it, too. "Maybe his real mom and dad wouldn't want him to practice all the time," Erin said. "Not if it makes him feel like moping around out on that porch."

She waited for the scolding that was sure to come.

"As I said, we'd better talk about it," Mr. Lindsay said. "You may have something there, Erin."

Her mother sat up straight. "Well, there's one more thing to talk about before we try to put this behind us," she said sternly, and Erin knew The Question was coming at last. "How did you know Cowper was out there on the porch, young lady? Surely you weren't aware he'd been taking this dreadful chance right along!"

This time it was Cowper who spoke up unexpectedly. "She didn't know," he said. "She's just a good guesser, that's all. I dared her to go out once, but she was chicken."

Erin's eyes widened. He was actually covering for her.

"Well, you should have told us he was even thinking about it, Erin," Mrs. Lindsay said tiredly. She sighed and stood up. "Next time you listen to your big sister, Cowper," she said. "Obviously, she has a lot more sense than you have."

Mr. Lindsay glanced at his watch, and then he jumped up, too.

"Good grief, Erin, your Miss Panca has been sitting downstairs waiting all this time!" he exclaimed. Then he frowned, remembering. "What brought you back up here, anyway?"

Erin tried to think of the right words to tell them. "She's not waiting," she said. Haltingly, she described her meeting with Mr. Barnhart.

When she'd finished, her mother and father put their arms around her. "We're so sorry, dear," her mother said. "You've lost a good friend. I know you'll miss her."

"Darn shame!" her father said gruffly.

Later, when Erin was alone in the living room, she went to the window and stared out. Darkness had closed in, hiding Kirby Avenue. Erin wondered if Molly's family were at their window, too.

I'll remember all of you forever, she promised. *And I'll remember tonight.*

Without a single ghost or witch, without a goblin or a vampire or a werewolf, it had definitely been the scariest night of her life.

Chapter Eighteen

"You've hated that dress ever since Aunt Gina sent it to you," Mrs. Lindsay said. "You don't like pink and you don't like ruffles. You didn't even want me to pack it when we were getting ready to come to Milwaukee. Why do you want to wear it today?"

Erin looked at herself in the full-length mirror bolted to her closet door. Molly Panca would have liked this dress. She would have loved it. And Molly would have liked the cluster of artificial lilies-of-the-valley pinned in Erin's hair.

"It's all right," she said. "Just this once."

Mrs. Lindsay looked doubtful. "It isn't the best choice for a funeral, dear. People usually wear dark clothes to funerals, you know. Your navy blue skirt would be more—"

"Molly liked pink and ruffles and lots of flowers," Erin said firmly. "She wouldn't like navy blue at all."

Two days had passed since Molly's death and Cowper's narrow escape. Two very peculiar days, Erin thought. She'd been sad, and lonely, too, when she thought about Molly. But the rest of the time she'd felt oddly light, like a helium balloon straining to fly away.

Today only one thing was important; she wanted to do what Molly Panca would have wanted. The Lindsays had already sent a spray of carnations and lilies to the funeral home. Molly would have appreciated that. And they were going to take Mr. Barnhart with them to the funeral. Molly would have been pleased about that, too.

"I think I'll sign up for the drama group at the Y," Erin said. (The helium-balloon feeling again, only now it had escaped and was bouncing against the ceiling.) "I'll do it tomorrow."

Mrs. Lindsay sat down on the studio couch. "Why now?" she demanded. "After all this time?"

"I thought you wanted me to do it," Erin told her. "You said—"

"I know what I said. Of course I want you to get out of the apartment and have some fun this summer. I'd just like to know what finally changed your mind. Was it Molly? Did she tell you to stop feeling sorry for yourself?"

"She never said I was feeling sorry for myself!" Erin exclaimed hotly. "Not once!"

"But she did want you to do *something* this summer, didn't she?" Mrs. Lindsay persisted.

She wanted Margaret Mary to do something. Erin turned away from the mirror and the pink, beruffled stranger looking out at her. "Molly never told me what to do," she said. She was beginning to feel trapped. The idea about going to the Y had just popped out, and now she was stuck with it. Strangely, though, the prospect didn't seem as impossible as it had before.

"Well, whatever the reason, I'm delighted." Mrs. Lindsay was smiling as she left the bedroom.

A moment later Cowper stopped at the door and peered in at her.

"You look weird," he said. "Honest."

Erin stuck out her tongue at him. "Listen," she said, "when we go home, I'll teach you how to skateboard, okay?"

Cowper's face went blank the way it always did when he was thinking hard. "Why?" he asked.

Erin smoothed a layer of pink ruffles. "Because otherwise you'll never learn. Do you think I want every kid in the park to know my brother is a klutz?"

"Uncle Jack and Aunt Grace won't let me," Cowper said. "They'll think I'm going to break a finger or something."

"They'll let you," Erin told him. "I heard them talking after you went to bed last night. Dad said you'd better finish up the master class this summer because we're here and everything, but when we go back to Clinton he wants you to stop lessons for a while. He says you're depressed. He said you're going to do just what you want to do for a year and only play the piano when you feel like it."

"What did Aunt Grace say?"

"She didn't like it, but she said okay. So do you want me to teach you or don't you?"

Cowper's expression was still carefully blank, but his eyes sparkled. "I guess—if you promise you won't wear that dress again." He continued down the hall, ignoring the pillow Erin threw at him.

Right then Erin knew why she felt so different, so runaway-balloon light. She'd feel the same no matter what happened to Cowper's career. For a few minutes Friday night she'd been certain he was dead and that it was all her fault. She had wanted to die, too. And then he'd come back. She'd been given a second chance to be—well, not a perfect Sara Crewe but a pretty good Erin Lindsay. A pretty good big sister.

There was a knock at the apartment door and murmuring voices in the front hall.

"Erin," Mrs. Lindsay called, "someone is here to see you."

Erin hurried down the hall. A tall, gray-haired woman stood just inside the door with a tissue-wrapped package in her arms.

"This is Miss Panca—Miss Doris Panca," Erin's
mother explained. "She's Molly's niece. She came all
the way from Phoenix for the funeral and to see about
Molly's apartment."

"My aunt must have been very fond of you, Erin,"
the visitor said. "She wanted you to have this." She
thrust the package into Erin's arms with a sweet Molly-
like smile.

They went into the living room, and Erin sat on the
couch to open her gift. Lily-white fabric spilled out as
she lifted Margaret Mary from the tissue and set her
carefully against the pillow.

"Oh my, what a lovely doll!" Mrs. Lindsay exclaimed. "Are you sure—?"

"There's a note," Molly's niece said. "See? It's pinned
to her sleeve. 'For Erin Lindsay, Apartment 508.' "

Erin gulped. "Where was she?" she asked. "Was she
up on the closet shelf?"

Mrs. Lindsay frowned, but Miss Panca didn't seem
to think it was a strange question. "No, as a matter of
fact she was sitting right in the middle of Aunt Molly's
bed, and all the other dolls were in a circle around her."

"She was telling them a story," Erin said. "She tells
wonderful stories." She straightened Margaret Mary's
bonnet and then slipped the little white traveling case
from the doll's arm. When she opened it, a scrap of
paper fluttered to the floor.

Mrs. Lindsay scooped it up. "I do believe it's a message for you, Erin. The handwriting is very shaky, but I can make it out: 'Here's a friend to talk to while you're—' " She turned the paper over and looked up in dismay. "She didn't finish it, I'm afraid. What a shame!"

" 'Here's a friend to talk to while you're making good things happen,' " Erin said. "That's how it was supposed to end."

It seemed to her that when she said that, Margaret Mary's pouty lips lifted, just a little, in a smile. "Don't be weird," Cowper would say, but she didn't care. The wonderful flyaway-balloon feeling was stronger than ever.

About the Author

BETTY REN WRIGHT is the author of many popular books for middle readers, including *The Dollhouse Murders*, which was a *Booklist* Editors' Choice; and *Christina's Ghost* and *Ghosts Beneath Our Feet*, which were both IRA-CBC Children's Choices.

Ms. Wright, an enthusiastic grandmother, lives in Wisconsin with her husband, painter George Frederickson, and their cat and dog.

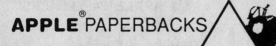